QUARRY's
DEAL

Books *by* Max Allan Collins

QUARRY

QUARRY'S LIST

QUARRY'S DEAL

QUARRY'S CUT

QUARRY'S VOTE

from PERFECT CRIME BOOKS

QUARRY's DEAL

MAX ALLAN COLLINS

With an Afterword by the Author

PERFECT CRIME BOOKS

Baltimore

Printed in the United States of America.

Perfect Crime Books is a registered Trademark.

Cover Design and Illustration © 2010 by Terry Beatty.

Library of Congress Cataloging-in-Publication Data
Collins, Max Allan
Quarry's Deal/Max Allan Collins
ISBN: 978-1-935797-03-6

This is for the cartoonist

Ray Gotto

whose "Ozark Ike" was a hitman, too.

"They gotta be taught to respeck us wommenfolks!"

Sagebrush Sal, 1948

1

I WAITED FOR her to come, and when she did, so did I. I asked her to lift and she lifted and let me get my hands out from under her. Here I'd been cupping that ass of hers, enjoying that fine ass of hers, and then we both came and suddenly her ass weighs a ton and all I can think about is getting my hands out from under before they get the fuck crushed.

I rolled off her.

"Was it good for you?" she asked.

"It was fine."

There was a moment of strained silence. She wanted me to ask, so I did: "How was it for you?"

"Fine," she said.

That taken care of, I got off the bed, slipped into my swim

trunks, trudged into her kitchen, and got myself a bottle of Coke.

"Get some kleenex for me," she called from the bedroom.

I was still in the kitchen. I said, "You want something to drink?"

"Please! Fix me a Seven and Seven, will you?"

Jesus, I thought. I put some Seagram's and Seven-Up and ice in a glass, got her some kleenex from the bathroom, and went into the bedroom, where she took both from me, setting the glass on the night-stand, stuffing the kleenex between her legs.

There was a balcony off the bedroom, through French doors, and I went out and looked down on the swimming pool below. It was mid-evening, and cool. Florida days are warm year round, they say, but the nights are on the chilly side, particularly a March one like this.

Not that the crowd of pleasure-seekers below seemed to mind. Or notice. Lean tan young bodies, of either sex, their privates covered by a slash or two of cloth, basked in the flickering glow of the torch lamps surrounding the pool. Some of them lounged on towels and sun chairs as if the full moon, which I could see reflected in the shimmery green water of the pool, was going to add to their already berry-brown complexions. Others romped, running around the pool's edge or in the water splashing, perpetual twelve-year-olds seeking perpetual summer.

I watched one well-endowed young woman tire of playing water baby with a boyfriend, climb out of the pool, tugging casually at her flimsy top which had slipped down to reveal dark half-circles of nipple. She was laughing, tossing back a headful of wet dark blond hair, shoving at the brawny chest of the guy who was climbing out of the pool after her. He pretended to be overpowered by her nudge and waved his arms and made a show of falling back in, but she no longer seemed amused.

She wasn't beautiful, exactly. The girl in the bedroom behind me was more classically beautiful, with a perfect, high-cheekboned fashion model face and a slim but well-proportioned figure. A lot of the girls at this place (which was an apartment complex for so-called "swinging singles") were the model type; others were more All-American-style beauties, sunny-faced girls sung about in songs by the Beach Boys. She fit neither type.

Her face was rather long, her nose long and narrow, her eyes having an almost oriental slant to them. Her mouth was wide and when she smiled, gums showed. Her figure was wrong, too: she was tall, at least an inch taller than my five ten, with much too lanky a frame for those huge breasts. Put that all together and she should have been a goddamn freak.

But she wasn't. The big breasts rode firm and high; she carried them well. Her face was unique-looking. You might say haunting. The eyes especially, which were dark blue with flecks of gold. Her voice was unusual, too—a rich baritone as deep as a man's, as deep as mine, in fact—but for some reason it only made her seem all the more feminine.

I didn't know her, but I knew who she was. I was here because of her. I'd been here, watching her, for almost a week now. If she noticed me, she gave no indication. Not that it mattered. The beard and mustache, once shaved off, would make me someone else; when we met in another context, one day soon, she'd have little chance of recognizing me, even if she had managed to pick me out of this crowd (which incidentally included several other beards and plenty of mustaches, despite the unspoken rule that tenants were to be on the clean-cut side in appearance, if not in behavior).

I hoped I wouldn't have to kill her. I probably would. But I hoped not. I'd never killed a woman before, though I didn't suppose it would be a problem. Only I hadn't counted on her looking like this. Her picture had made her look almost homely. I'd had no idea she radiated this aura of some goddamn thing or another, some damn thing that made me want to know her, made me uncomfortable at the thought of having to kill her.

"Hey," she said.

I turned.

This one's name was Nancy. She was wearing a skimpy black bikini. She had short dark black hair and looked like a fashion model. Or did I mention that already?

"You want to go down and swim?" she asked.

"Later," I said.

"Is that Coke good?"

"It's fine."

"How come you don't drink anything but Coke and that? Got something against liquor?"

"No. I have a mixed drink sometimes."

"What d'you come out here for?"

"It's nice out here."

"Is it because you knew I'd smoke?"

"I guess."

"Don't you have a single fucking vice?"

"Not one."

"Tell me something."

"Okay."

"You always this blue after you do it?"

"Just sometimes."

"Every time. With me, anyway. You always get all, uh, what's a good word for it?"

"Quiet."

4

"No. Morose. That's the word I want."

"Quiet is what I get. Don't read anything into anything, Nancy."

"I knew a guy like you once. He always got . . . quiet . . . after doing it."

"Is that right."

"You know what he said once?"

"No."

"He said, 'Doing it is like Christmas: after all the presents are open, you can't remember what the fuss was all about.'" And she laughed, but it got caught in her throat.

"What are you depressed for?"

"I'm not depressed. Don't read anything into anything, Burt."

Burt is the name I was using here. I thought it sounded like a good swinging singles name.

"My husband used to get sad, sometimes, after we did it."

Him again. She talked about him all the time, her ex. About what a son of a bitch he was, mostly. He was an English professor at some eastern university, with rich parents who underwrote him, He (or rather they) paid for Nancy's apartment here in Florida. There was a kid, too, a daughter I think, living with Nancy's parents in Michigan.

"You know what he used to say?" she asked.

"Something about Christmas?"

"No. He used to say that in France coming is called the little death."

"That's a little over my head, Nancy."

"Well, he was an intellectual. The lousy prick. But I think what it means is when you come, it's like dying for a second, you're going out of this life into some place different. You're not thinking about money or your problems or anything. All you can think of is coming. And you aren't thinking about that, either. You're just coming."

Down by the pool, the girl I'd come here to watch was sitting along the edge, kicking at the water, while her blond boyfriend tried to kid her out of her mood.

Nancy's hand was on my shoulder. I looked at her and she was lifting her mouth up to me, which meant I was supposed to kiss her, and I did. I put my hand between her legs and nudged her with a finger.

"Bang," I said.

She took my arm and pulled me into the bedroom.

2

WE WENT DOWN for a swim afterwards. I let Nancy do the swimming. I like to swim, but I don't like crowds. You can't swim in a crowd. All you can do is wade around bumping into people. So Nancy swam and I watched.

I didn't watch Nancy, though. I just pretended to. What my eyes were really on was the young woman with the big breasts and oriental eyes and muscle-bound boyfriend. The boyfriend had the look of a Hollywood glamour boy gone slightly to seed. Thinning hair; puffy face; on the road to a paunch.

She was bored with him. He'd given up trying to talk her out of her indifference to him and was sitting in a beach chair with a drink in his hands, watching a blonde in a yellow bikini who sat across the way looking as bored with her companion as the big-breasted oriental-eyed girl was bored with him.

I was bored, too. I hadn't been here a week and I was suffocating. I live in Wisconsin, near the Lake Geneva vacation center, and the summer months around those parts are cherished and enjoyed and, in the freezing cold winter months, looked forward to. I'd come here expecting a similar attitude. Instead I found the year-round summer was not so much taken for granted as squandered. Made meaningless.

I never imagined yards of beautiful exposed flesh under sunny skies could get dull. I never thought cool evenings full of cool drinks and warm glances could grow monotonous. I never dreamed sex could become so tedious.

Nancy wanted it every time I turned around. Three or four times a day, and the first couple days I was glad to accommodate. I'd gone for months without getting laid, and was more than ready. But after close to a week of it, I was just plain tired. The crazy part was what Nancy told me about the breakup of her marriage: "The son of a bitch was a sex maniac. . . . He didn't respect me as a person at all." She told me this while we were taking a shower together.

All of this was new to me. I had never had to maintain a relationship with one woman while watching another woman I would most likely have to kill. I was used to keeping those two particular compartments of my life separate. I led a relatively normal social life in Wisconsin, including an occasional Nancy. But the life away from home was something else again. The business part of my life, I mean. The killing.

Of course I was in a different business now; slightly different, anyway. A new, self-created business that would require an intermixing, now and then, of the social me and the other one.

And I was finding out now, in my first time out, that playing both roles at once could prove to be a little disturbing.

Or anyway, irritating.

Though considering the boredom of this would-be paradise, a touch of irritation was maybe a good thing. At least I was awake. Aware, always, I was here on business. Perhaps I should've been thankful I hadn't been seduced by the sex-and-sun, flesh-and-fun atmosphere of the place.

Only I was finding something else irritating. Or disturbing, anyway. I had developed a nagging fascination with the woman I was watching, that oriental-eyed woman with the big breasts, a woman who didn't seem to quite fit in here, and that fascination was unhealthy as hell, especially since this was my first outing in my new (make that revised) line of work.

How much longer was I going to have to watch her? Another week? A month? Longer? I never have liked stakeout work, and this swinging singles lifestyle, with its fringe "benefit" of constant sex, seemed likely to kill me before I had a chance to kill anybody myself.

Maybe tonight would be different. After all, the afternoon had been different. The tall, busty woman I'd been watching these past few days had acted a little strange this afternoon. All week she'd been giddy, just another bubble-headed fun-seeker playing footsy and everything-elsey with her blond boyfriend. But this afternoon she'd gotten moody. Her face had taken on an almost grim look. Her efforts at having fun seemed just that: efforts. Efforts that had failed and lapsed into . . . what? Depression? No. More like seriousness. A serious mood, rather than a black or bitchy one.

Something was up, maybe.

Not me, certainly: I was wilted. Nancy was going to have to learn to respect me as a person—for the rest of the night, anyway.

Meanwhile the crowd in and around the pool was beginning to thin. Nancy begged off around two-thirty and by that time there was only half a dozen of us left. My dragon lady was one. Her blond hunk of manhood was another, only now he was in the water with a blond hunk of womanhood whose own hunk she had managed to lose, along with the top of her bikini, and two small but perfectly shaped boobs bobbled in the water like apples, pink apples, if there is such a thing, or even if there isn't. I didn't much care either way. I was too wrung out to care. Not so the two blonds: they climbed out of the pool giggling and one chased the other into the shadows.

That left me alone with her.

Which was not good. A harmless conversation, idly struck . . . and the ballgame was over. Of course there was a whole pool between us; better an ocean. I needed to stay just some anonymous bearded guy who she had never really looked at close, otherwise the entire deal was blown.

But she wasn't looking at me. She was looking at the water. Staring at it, the surface rippling with the slight breeze, the torch lights shimmering eerily in reflection.

And then she got up and went up the open stairway to the second level, where her apartment was.

I stayed behind. I was, to say the least, relieved. And now that I had the pool to myself, I could have a nice, private swim, which is a daily ritual of mine, whenever possible, anyway.

I dove in.

I'd just swum my sixth easy lap when she came down wearing a dark, mannish pants suit, suitcase in either hand, and headed into the parking lot, from which, moments later, came the sound of squealing tires.

3

I COULD HAVE followed her. I had my car keys in the pocket of my robe, which was with my towel, under the beach chair where I'd been sitting before I started my swim.

But I might have looked just a shade conspicuous jumping into the Opel GT soaking wet, in nothing but a pair of swim trunks, and considering I was already afraid she might have taken some notice of me, following her, at this moment, in my present condition, didn't seem, well, prudent.

The next best thing to following her was to find out where she was going.

So that's what I decided to do. Try to do, anyway.

I hadn't ever gotten in her apartment to look around, despite the number of days I'd been there. She hadn't left the grounds of the place since I'd arrived: she sent her boyfriend out to do the grocery shopping, and with all the drinking and sex available on the premises, who needed to go out for anything except supplies?

I maybe could have got in and searched her place while she was down by the pool with her blond plaything; she did spend a lot of time down there, after all, but who was to say when she or the plaything might tire of the pool and come up for a nap or something. And, too, during all but a few of the nocturnal hours, I was playing plaything myself, for Nancy, so when the fuck was I supposed to get in that apartment for a look?

Now.

Now I could do it. The dragon lady was gone, packed and left in the middle of the night, as a matter of fact, and her boyfriend was apparently shacked up, at least temporarily, with a new mistress . . . and I don't mean mistress in the modern sense, not exactly.

I mean mistress in the dictionary sense, "woman in authority, in control." Women ruled at that place. It should've been called-the Amazon Arms (and not Beach Shore Apartments, which is redundant as hell, I know, but then the owner/manager's name was Bob Roberts, so you figure it). The Beach Shore rented exclusively to women. Divorced women, mostly, alimony-rich divorced women.

All the rooms had double beds, and there were a lot of men around, but the men would come and go, so to speak, and the women stayed on.

Which is why it hadn't been hard to infiltrate the place. I just dropped in one afternoon and sat by the pool, wearing my tight little trunks, and waited to be picked up. It wasn't as degrading as I'd imagined it, but it was degrading enough. As any woman reading this could tell you.

So now that the dragon lady was away, with an apparent

rift developed between her and her plaything, I figured I'd find that apartment very empty. And the risk of being interrupted while I had my look around was little or no.

Getting in would be no problem. Getting in was never a problem around this place, in about any sense you can think of. The asshole who managed the place (the owner, old Bob Roberts, remember?) was never in his own apartment, as he considered that part of his function was servicing any of his tenants who were momentarily between playthings. He liked to tell his tenants his door was always open, and it was. So was his fly.

Anyway, I walked in one afternoon, found his master key in a drawer and took it to a Woolworth's in the nearby good-size town, where I had a dupe made, returned his key, and got back in bed with Nancy, all in the course of fifty minutes.

I used to be good at picking locks, but got out of the habit. For what I'd been doing the past few years, I'd seldom needed tools of that sort, as most of my work was in the Midwest, where security tends to be lax, where most doors can be opened with a credit card, and there are lots of other ways to get in a place if you have to, easier ways than picking a lock, I mean, which honest-to-Christ requires daily practice. Anybody tells you picking locks is easy is somebody who doesn't know how to pick locks.

I got out of the pool.

I put on my robe, went up the steps and inside, where I found the corridor empty and felt no apprehension at all as I worked the dupe of the owner/manager's master key in the lock and went in. I turned on the lights (the windows of her apartment faced the ocean-front side of the building, so no one was likely to see them on, and even so, so what?) and began poking around.

The apartment itself was identical in layout to Nancy's, except backwards, as this was on the opposite side of the hall. The decorating was very different, which surprised me: apparently each tenant could have her own decorating done, so where a wall in Nancy's had pastel blue wallpaper, light color blue like Wisconsin summer sky, the dragon lady had shiny metallic silver wallpaper; other walls were standard dark paneling in either apartment, but in this one, for example, a gleaming metal bookcase-cum-knickknack rack jutted across the living room, cutting it in half, with few books on it and a lot of weird African-looking statues and some abstract sculptures made of glazed black something. And where in Nancy's place there was a lot of wood, nothing furniture, everything antiques, this place had plastic furniture, metal furniture, glass furniture, all of it looking expensive and cheap at the same time.

In the bedroom, above the round waterbed, with its white silk sheets and black furry spread, was a painting. A black square with an immense red dot all but engulfing it. Nancy had a picture above her bed, too. An art nouveau print of a beautiful woman in a flowing scarf against a pastel background. Nancy had an antique brass bed. I had the feeling these girls weren't two of a kind.

Meanwhile, I was going through things. The name she was using here was Glenna Cole, but I found identification cards of various sorts in several other names. The Broker's name for her was Ivy. Knowing Broker's so-called sense of humor, that probably came from poison ivy. Broker called me Quarry. Because (he said) a quarry is carved out of rock. The Broker's dead now.

I found a gun. A spare, probably. She wouldn't have taken her suitcases with her unless she was going off on a job. That was my guess, anyway, and it came from experience. Also, the gun was just a little purse thing, a pearl-handled .22 automatic, and I imagined she used something a little heavier than that in her work. A .38, at least. Speaking of which, I did find a box of .38 shells behind some lacy panties in a drawer, and that substantiated my guesswork, as there was no gun here that went with these shells.

What I didn't find was evidence of where she'd gone. I went through the wastebaskets, and I even went through a bag of garbage in her kitchen, and found nothing, no plane or bus reservation notice, no nothing. I even played the rubbing a pencil against the top blank sheet of a note pad trick, and while it seems to work on television, all I got for my trouble was dirty fingers.

I sat on an uncomfortable-looking comfortable couch in her living room and wondered what to do next.

That was when her boyfriend came in.

4

I SAID, "WHO the hell are you?"

His mouth dropped open like a trap door.

"So who the hell are you?" I demanded again.

He cocked his head like a dog trying to comprehend its master, narrowing his eyes, making them seem more close-set than they really were.

"Well?" I said.

That's the only way I know to handle a situation like that: turn the tables, put the shoe on the other foot, or whatever other cliché you want to use to describe what I was doing to him. It was the only way I knew that might avoid immediate violence. I don't care for physical violence myself, and try to duck it whenever possible.

Especially when faced with a guy both bigger and

stronger than me, facts made obvious by his standing there in swim trunks and towel, the latter flung casually over a classically muscular shoulder.

"Well, are you coming in or aren't you?" I asked.

He pushed the door shut. His teeth were showing. He wasn't smiling. But he was too confused to be violent. At the moment.

"I don't know you," he said.

"If I knew you," I said, "would I be asking your goddamn name every couple seconds?"

His eyebrows were as light a blond as the hair on his head. His nose was small, almost feminine. He really was prettier-looking than the dragon lady. But nowhere near as interesting.

"You got a reason for being in Glenna's room?" he said. His voice was medium-range, flat, uninteresting.

"Sure. Do you?"

"Yeah. Yeah, I do. I live here."

"The hell you say." I knew he did, of course, had seen the men's clothing in the closet and in dresser drawers, and knew of the female domination of the place which meant any man here was living with whatever woman he served. What I didn't know was how fast this asshole was, that he'd pull a wham/bam/thank-you-ma'am on that female counterpart of himself he'd gone off into the shadows with. I mean, even at the Beach Shore you spent the night with whoever you banged. Sometimes you stayed the month.

"Hey," he said, sitting in a chair across from me, a glass coffee table separating us. "Hey, I've seen you someplace. You staying here with somebody? Have I seen you down by the pool?"

"I'm staying here. You might have seen me."

"But we haven't met."

"That's right."

"I'm Norm Morrow."

"Burt Thompson."

We didn't shake hands, by the way.

"Okay, then. Okay, Burt. Now we're introduced. Now maybe you don't mind going into what you're doing in here?"

"I'm waiting for Glenna."

"Glenna's gone."

"She'll be back."

"Not for a while, bud."

"I'll wait a while. And it's Burt."

"I don't give a fuck it's Henry Kissinger. I'm starting to get the idea you're fucking around with me, and I don't like it."

"If you hadn't gone fucking around with some other piece of ass but Glenna, maybe she wouldn't have asked me up here."

"That's horseshit, pal."

"How so?"

"Glenna doesn't give a damn what I do while she's gone, she's gone sometimes a month at a time, and she doesn't expect me to be a fucking priest, you know? It's an understanding we got. And I'm beginning to understand something else. . . . I had about enough of you. Now what is this *really* about?"

"All I know is she asked me up, asked me to stay on, maybe she just figured I'd pass the word onto you your welcome was worn out . . ."

"Hey. You were just leaving, sport."

"I don't want any trouble. You're a whole lot stronger than me, I can see that. No need to go proving it."

"So get the fuck out of here, then."

"Look, why don't we just ask Glenna which of us she wants to hang around."

"What? She split, she's gone, hasn't that sunk in yet, you jackass?"

"We'll call her and ask her."

"I don't have a number to reach her, and neither do you."

"I admit I don't. I just thought maybe you did. You say you live here."

"Well . . . sometimes she leaves a number."

"Yeah?"

"I don't know why I'm playing along with you on this, I really don't . . ."

"We'll call. Come on."

"She won't be there till tomorrow, at least. She's driving, and it's a long way where she's headed."

"Where's that?"

"You're her new boyfriend and you don't know? Hey. That's all. That's all I can take. Just haul your ass off that couch and get outa here. Okay?"

I was admiring a metallic abstract sculpture on the glass coffee table between us. It was egg-shaped, the sculpture, with an indentation on either side, and about the size of a baseball, a little taller maybe. When I hit him with it, he went down without a sound. He missed the table, landed soft on the tufts of shag carpet. I hit him again, once, in the same spot, and made sure the skull was cracked open.

One good thing was he landed on his right side and it was his left side I'd hit, the left side of his head I mean, so there wasn't any blood on the carpet, and wouldn't be if I moved him quick and careful.

I left him in the bathtub, after pulling off his trunks, heaving him in, turning on the shower, and leaving him looking like he'd slipped and fallen in there, cracking his head open against the side of the tub.

The work of art I wrapped in a towel and took with me, for later disposal.

The telephone number she left him I found under the phone.

5

KILLING PEOPLE WITH blunt objects isn't really my style, but then style is a luxury I can't always indulge in. Carrying on a conversation with somebody I know I'm going to have to kill isn't my style, either. Under ideal conditions I'd just walk in, without a word, use my gun, and go. Hello, goodbye.

But conditions aren't always ideal. Sometimes conditions are pure shit. And being able to adapt to an unforeseen, shit situation is what separates the men from the boys, the living from the dead. Being able to adapt and survive.

That I learned in Vietnam. I learned a lot of things in Vietnam, not the least of which was the meaninglessness of life and death, and the importance of survival. Those may not seem compatible, but they are. Only when you realize how little your life means, and how slender a thread it hangs on, do you begin to know the meaning of the word survival.

There's nobody easier to kill than a self-important man, a man who feels the world revolves around him, a man who finds it hard to imagine that maybe things would go on without him. For instance. Political assassinations. Everybody knows they happen every day, but there isn't a world leader living who wouldn't be shocked to be dying.

Of course that's an easy example. Everybody knows it's easier for a politician to grasp the possibility of a nuclear war ending the world than to understand that a bullet through his brain, say, could end a brilliant political career. And those of them that live through assassination attempts teach their crippled bodies to walk again so as to get back on the firing line as soon as possible.

I'll tell you who else is an easy mark: anybody sitting on the board of any corporation. Wouldn't have to be General Motors or U.S. Steel or anything. It could be the lowliest member of the board of the country's least successful condom company. There isn't a one of those assholes whose last words wouldn't be, "There must be some mistake."

But it's also the guy who's been smoking for twenty-five years and has a hacking cough and is short of wind but keeps on lighting up smoke after smoke, pack after pack, and when the doctor shows the guy the X-ray of what's left of his lungs, well, nobody could be more surprised.

Religious people are easy marks, too. They all think the fix is in.

It isn't. Not in this world, anyway.

For five years, more or less, I killed people for money. Good money, that is. Before that I'd done it for lousy money, for Uncle Sugar; and in one case, for free, when I got home from Nam and found my wife in bed with a guy named Williams, who I didn't kill on the spot, waiting a day to cool down and then going over to his house where he was in the driveway under his sporty little car and kicked the jack out. Sometimes I wish it had been my wife under there instead of that poor bastard Williams. Ex-wife, now. Anyway, it got some attention in the papers, which is probably how the Broker heard about me.

He'd picked a good time to come look me up. I'd spent I don't know how long, months maybe, looking for work, but between the publicity I'd got for murdering my wife's boyfriend, despite my acquittal, and the general bad reputation of returning Vietnam vets, who were considered poor risks for employment since all of us were crazed glassy-eyed dope addicts, I'd found nothing, nothing but a fleabag hotel room, a dose of clap from some hooker, and a visit from my old man who dropped by to tell me not to come back to Ohio because his latest wife was scared of me.

At any rate, he looked me up, the Broker did, and made me a business proposition which I accepted without hesitation. The Broker was a middle man in the murder business ; he provided insulation between client and killer. "Sort of an agent," he'd said. I was to be part of a team, a two-man team breaking down to active and passive, hitman and back-up. He felt I'd find the active role more to my liking. He was right.

He was right about a lot of things in those five years, though there had been one thing he was wrong about, but that's a long story, which I've recorded elsewhere, and it would be beyond the purpose of this present account to go into all of that again.

Suffice to say I'm alive and the Broker isn't. And I have the Broker's list.

It's a list running to approximately fifty names, fifty entries, each including extensive biographical information, current and previous addresses, photographs, and a record of each specific job carried out. I used to be on the list, but I removed and destroyed my entry as soon as the thing landed in my hands. But I'd been there. All of us were. All of the people like me who'd done work for the Broker.

(This is not to suggest any brotherhood, any bond, between myself and the others on the list. I'd only worked with a handful of them. My longtime partner, for instance, was dead.)

The Broker was by no means a unique entity; there were others like him. And by now most of the people on the list would be working again, carrying out new assignments for their new Brokers. Life goes on, after all. Death, too.

But for me there would be no more Brokers; no more middle men. No way.

I had the list.

And no desire to take over where the Broker left off, no intention of playing the middle man role myself and becoming what I'd come to hate. Nor did I have any intention of using the list to try and blackmail anyone on it. A hired killer isn't your ideal blackmail victim. Docile they aren't.

But suppose.

Suppose I were to pick a name off the list, pick a killer out of the Broker's hat. Suppose I were to follow that killer to his latest job, wait and watch and find out who his potential victim might be. And suppose I were to then go to that potential victim and tell him what's about to happen to him. And offer my help in the matter. Offer a little preventive medicine. For a fee.

It was a crazy idea.

But suppose it worked . . .

6

I BROUGHT THE razor up to my throat and stroked. A final patch of beard disappeared and the face looking back at me in the mirror was vaguely familiar.

And not a little strange. The upper part of my face was Florida tan, but the lower, newly bare half was pale as baby powder. I had grown the beard to change my appearance temporarily, assuming once the thing was off that my rather ordinary features would keep me a face in the crowd. Only not many faces in the crowd have two-tone complexions.

I shrugged at my familiar, strange reflection, thinking what the hell, I'll just have to take time out and do something about it.

I splashed some water on my face, a little sting of shave lotion, and walked naked out into the bedroom part of the motel room, where the television was going, a morning game show on, a woman dressed as a head of cabbage standing next to a man, presumably her husband, wearing a sort of perforated tin skirt. The host was asking him what he was supposed to be, and the guy was saying, "I grate." I couldn't have agreed more. I turned it off, got into my swim trunks, and went out to the pool.

It was eleven-thirty and the sun was almost to the middle of the sky, a nice hot sun that would take care of my facial problem no trouble. I found a beach chair near poolside, adjusted it to make sure I would get full benefit of the sun's rays, and leaned back, covering the top of my face with a towel.

I suppose I looked a little weird, but it didn't matter much, as there wasn't a soul around. It was a terrific place to spend a morning and afternoon. Finally, around three, a mother and her couple of kids took a quick dip, and then a bit later another mother and her teenage daughter came out for some sun. The teenage daughter was a sweet little thing, very slim but very pretty, and she smiled at me. I didn't smile back. I didn't want to encourage her. One thing I didn't need right now was sexual activity. That's what I was recovering from. I also didn't need an indignant mother, which can happen when you screw a teenage daughter, as it irks a middle-aged mother to discover her offspring is the more sexually attractive of the two.

I had left the Beach Shore early this morning, waking Nancy to tell her goodbye, as I didn't want to seem to be sneaking out. I had no idea when the body in the shower would be found, didn't expect it to be for several days at least, but at any rate I didn't want to make a suspicious exit. Nancy wasn't surprised to see me go. She was a little sad; she even managed a tear. Ours, apparently, had been one of her longer-lasting recent relationships.

I had made no attempt to make good time; in fact I had stopped mid-morning while still in Florida (barely) at this motel to get some rest, shave off my beard, do some thinking, and swim in a pool that wasn't populated with water bunnies of various sexes. Now that I had found out about the pale beneath my beard, I was especially glad I'd stopped while still in the sunny south. I tan easily, or rather burn easily, the burn turning to tan literally overnight. So by tomorrow I'd be a new man.

I knew where she was headed. Glenna Cole or Ivy or whatever you want to call her. All it had taken was a few minutes on the phone with a helpful operator. I merely said a message had been left for me, a request that I call this certain number and I wanted to find out the source of the number before returning the call. The operator had said it was against company policy to do that, and I said I didn't need a name or a street address, just the town would do fine. She gave me the town and I thanked her and when I hung up I had to laugh.

The name of the town the operator had given me was West Lake, Iowa.

I had picked Glenna Cole from my list because her permanent address was the Beach Shore in Florida. I had wanted to escape the Midwest, a Midwest which was still cold as hell though this was supposed to be spring, and break the rule and mix business with pleasure, get some sun, swim in the ocean, maybe get laid. In my desire to ease the boredom of working stakeout, I had chosen Florida, where I had not once been able to swim in the ocean, and where I got laid till I wanted to check into a monastery, and where I got so much sun half my face got tan.

And now I was heading back to the Midwest, back to

Iowa, for Christ's sake, where I'd just a few months ago been involved in a messy business that had put me in hiding until just a week and a half ago.

The messy business was this federal guy I shot. I didn't know he was federal at the time. I didn't know he was anything except a guy searching my hotel room, and he had a gun, which he started using when he saw me come in, so I used mine.

I never killed a federal agent before, or any kind of cop for that matter, at least that I know of. Finding out the guy was federal gave me a bad moment: I wondered if maybe it might not be hard to get away with.

But I was more worried about mob people, in whose affairs I'd been fiddling when I accidentally shot the federal guy. In fact that's who I thought I was shooting at the time, a mob guy. So I'd covered my tracks (pretty well, considering it was spur of the moment) and retreated, burrowed in, waited to see what happened next.

Nothing happened next. I just sat around all winter, in my A-frame cottage on Paradise Lake in Wisconsin, drinking Coke and watching television and listening to music and reading paperback novels and swimming once a day (at the YMCA at nearby Lake Geneva) and growing a beard.

And thinking. Thinking about the new role I was preparing to play, assuming some federal guys didn't come around to kill me. Or mob guys. Neither of which I intended to let happen, but in either case a change of plan would be called for.

By spring nobody had come around, so I figured I was okay. I picked a name off the Broker's list and got in my Opel GT and went to Florida.

And now I was on my way back to the Midwest. Or would be tomorrow.

Today I had to get half my face sunburned.

7

THE RED BARN Club was five miles out of West Lake, Iowa, on a blacktop road, or so I'd been told. So far all I'd seen were farms and farmland, the latter still patched with snow, the fields flat except for an occasional stubborn corn stalk hanging crookedly against the pale orange sky like a crutch in search of a cripple.

This was the end of my second day since leaving Florida. I'd done six hundred miles (give or take a hundred) both days, and had staggered into Des Moines earlier this afternoon, checking into a Holiday Inn which had a breathtaking view of the local freeway. The first thing I'd done after getting in my room was call the number I'd found in Glenna Cole's apartment at the Beach Shore. It didn't even take a long distance call: West Lake was one of a number of smaller towns in the surrounding area included in the Des Moines phone system.

The voice on the other end of the line was female, pleasantly so, and answered this way: "Red Barn Club, Lucille."

I bluffed. "Excuse me . . . I was calling the Red Barn restaurant."

"We are a restaurant, sir."

"Oh, well, I'm from out of town, in Des Moines for the night, and they tell me the Red Barn's a good place to eat, so . . ."

"Where are you calling from, sir?"

And I told her, and she gave me directions, which I followed, and now I was driving along a gently rolling black-top road, looking idly at farms and farmland, wondering where the hell this place was, anyway, and saw it.

And almost missed it.

The Red Barn was, of all things, a barn, a reconverted one to be sure, but driving by you could miss it easily, take it for just a freshly painted building where cows lived and hay was kept.

After the pleasant female voice on the phone, eagerly dispensing directions to the place, I hardly expected such a painstakingly anonymous establishment: The wide side of the barn facing the road had no identifying marks, no sign decorating that expanse of red-painted, white-trimmed wood: No lighting called attention to the structure, and there weren't any cars around. The only tip-off was the white picket fence gate, which was open and did have a small sign saying RED BARN CLUB. Why the low profile? I wondered. What was this a place where rich guys came to pay to fuck sheep?

Whatever the case, I was joining the fun. I eased the Opel GT down a wide paved drive beyond the gate, followed around to a large parking lot in back, large enough for several hundred cars, and presently about half full, and on a week night, no less. I parked as close to the door as I could, pulling in between a Ford LTD and a Cadillac. Mine was one of the few cars in the lot without a vinyl top. This place had something, apparently, that attracted a money crowd. Good-looking sheep, maybe.

There was some lighting back here, subdued, but lighting; and over the door, which was in the middle of the barn side, was a small sign, red neon letters on a white-painted wood field, just the initials: R B C. That was either class or snobbery, I wasn't sure which. I wasn't sure there was a difference.

The interior was a surprise. The lighting was low-key, as I'd expected, but it was a soft-focus sort of thing, gold-hued, glowing, not unlike the sunset I'd just witnessed.

The girl who greeted me at the door was glowing, too. A honey-haired young woman with a bustline you could balance drinks on. She was wearing a sleeveless clinging red sweater and high-waisted denim slacks and a beaming smile. The smile was phony, but she was good at it. And the bustline was real, so who cared?

"Are you a club member, sir?"

I said I wasn't. I said I was from out of town. Which was a little moronic, since the Red Barn Club wasn't in a town.

"Will you just be dining with us, then, sir?"

"I guess so," I said.

And was led up some stairs into the dining room. I hadn't had time to absorb the entryway I'd been standing in, having been confronted with all that honey-colored hair and teeth and tits, but I did have time to notice a closed door at the bottom of a short flight of steps off on the right from the entry landing.

But I was going upstairs, not down, and I was in a dining room, a surprisingly folksy one, at that. The decor was western and about as authentic as a Roy Rogers movie. Like the exterior, the walls were painted red with white trim. The dining room was separated into four rows of booths, a row against each wall, two rows side by side down the middle of the room, each booth made out of bare rough wood, picket-fence sides, crosshatched beams for roofs. The rustic effect was offset by plastic flowers on plastic vines twined around the front roof beam of each booth.

I was in one of the side booths, next to a window, which had shutters below and ruffled, red-and-white checked curtains above. The curtains matched the tablecloths. I was wondering if I could see the parking lot from where I sat, but the shutters proved to be permanently closed.

I wanted to look out over the cars in the lot and see if I could spot a certain one.

Glenna Cole, or Ivy (as my late friend the Broker had called her), drove a light blue Stingray. Of course she might have changed cars en route, but not necessarily. It was worth checking, anyway.

I was standing up in the booth, peeking out through the ruffled curtains, when the waitress came, a girl less busty but equally as attractive as the honey-haired greeter at the door. She too was wearing the red sweater and denim slacks combination, which proved to be the uniform of all the young women working at the Red Barn Club.

I ordered, spent some time trying to look out the window at the lot, to no avail, and the food came, and was nothing special. The specialty was nothing special, in fact: barbeque ribs that were okay but that's all. Salad, hash browns, bread, all of it okay. Nothing more.

Outside of whoever hired the waitresses being a good

judge of pulchritude, the Red Barn didn't seem to me to have what it took to attract a hundred or so cars on a Thursday night. But that's how many cars were out there.

Only how many people were in here?

A few couples, some foursomes, everyone dressed casually (I was the only person in the room with a coat and tie on). Twenty-four people, maybe. Figure ten cars, at the most.

I had the waitress bring me a Coke from the bar and I sat and drank it.

Then I went down to find out what was behind that closed door.

8

IT WAS A room full of tables. The walls were that same barn
red with white trim, but there was a noticeable absence of
decoration. Only at the far end, which was given over to the
bar, was the mock western motif of the upper floor
continued: horse-collar mirrors; some western paintings;
chairs made from the same rough wood as the picket fence
booths upstairs; tables that were glass-covered wagon
wheels. But that was just in the bar area. Throughout the
rest of the room the walls were bare, the tables were
cardtables, round, the chairs metal folding type with
padded backs and seats.

It was also a room full of people. The cars in the
parking lot now seemed justified, and then some. There
wasn't an empty seat in the house, though I felt sure one

would be found, and room made, at any table I might care to join.

There was one small area of the room that was unlit, with several long tables which were covered. This, I learned from a waitress, was where the roulette and craps was played, on the weekends. Week nights, only the card tables were open.

This wasn't Las Vegas, but for a place stuck between a couple of Iowa cornfields it was close enough. It certainly lacked the trappings of Las Vegas, excluding the showgirl-pretty waitresses, who went around keeping the customers well-lubricated, but all of it went on the bill, none of your free drinks stuff here, and instead of chips, the players used money, stacks of it littered each table, paper money, and not that multicolor stuff they use in Monopoly, either: the real, green thing.

To be in this room you had to be a member. I was a member. I had just paid ten dollars for an out-of-town membership. Des Moines area members paid ten dollars, too. Membership was lifetime. The little brown card, which I was required to sign, said so. Considering the kind of stakes in question here, ten bucks was a drop in a bucket so deep you wouldn't hear the drop.

I played blackjack for a while. For half an hour. I lost fifty bucks without trying. I went from there to a table where they were playing five-card stud and lasted five hands, throwing away twenty-five bucks on nothing but anteing up.

I shouldn't have chosen blackjack, which is my worst game, or five-card stud either, my second worst. I shouldn't have been playing cards at all, coming off of two days of solid driving, which had left me sluggish to say the least, and one thing I didn't need to spend any more time in was a sitting position. What I did need was a bed. I was getting sleepy just thinking about it.

But this place, this Red Barn Club with its hokey decor and mediocre restaurant and high stakes gambling set-up, was where my dragon lady, Glenna Cole, had gone. Or anyway, where simple reasoning said she'd gone, considering the Barn's phone number was the one she'd left for her (late) lover.

So I needed to get the feel of the place, find out what it was about, find out what was going on here that could require the specialized talents of the beautiful Ms. Cole.

By the time I'd settled in at a table where three-card draw poker (jacks or better to open, progressive ante) was being played, I had traversed the room and pretty well convinced myself Glenna Cole was not around, not anywhere where I could see her, anyway.

I was beginning to think I'd beat her here. I hadn't made great time on my way up from Florida, but not terrible time, either, and maybe she'd made a side trip or something.

If she *was* here, she'd be easy enough to spot. The oriental eyes, the awesome breasts, how could you miss her? Even if the room were full of women.

Which it wasn't. There were a few ladies mixed in at the blackjack tables, several others playing casino, just one or two playing at a poker table where a handsome young house dealer was offering seven-card stud. The week nights at the Barn, it would seem, belonged primarily to area businessmen having a night out; the weekends apparently attracted more couples, from the area and outside of it too, probably, with the craps and roulette tables being better suited to the needs of a mixed crowd.

At any rate, if Glenna Cole was among the few females present, she was wearing a hell of a disguise. Outside of the waitresses, these were women in their forties, wives,

divorcees, maybe a mistress or two. Too much make-up. Expensive, ugly pants suits. A hell of a disguise.

The men were dressed more casually, country club casual, sports shirts, knit slacks, occasionally a sport coat, seldom a tie. This included the house dealers, who, unlike the waitresses, wore no specific uniform.

The house dealer at the draw poker table was a guy in his early twenties with short black hair, glasses, and a worried expression. He was the weakest dealer in the room, easy, and I started winning off him right away. Most of the dealers were making cheerful, if terse, conversation with the patrons, but this kid was tightlipped, bordering on sullen.

I was up a hundred and a half after less than an hour, and a guy across from me at the table (there were five of us in) was up maybe two hundred. He was a fat guy in a striped shirt with a string tie that had a little calf's head choker; whether or not he'd dressed to suit the decor, or was just an asshole, I can't say. I'd guess the latter.

We were up to aces or better to open, second time around. The ante was five bucks, so there was a hundred seventy-five bucks in the pot before any betting started. I opened with aces, betting ten bucks. Everybody stayed. I drew three cards, picked up another ace. Everybody drew three except the fat guy, who drew to either a four-card flush or four-card straight; whichever it was, he didn't make it, and folded before the second round of betting could begin.

I threw another ten in and everybody dropped but the dealer. He raised me twenty-five, which was the limit. I raised him another twenty-five, and he swallowed, and called.

"Bullets," I said, and showed him the aces, two red ones and a spade.

He swallowed again, and his cards tumbled out of his fingers and I caught a glimpse of a king, and he raked the cards back in.

"Three kings, huh," I said. "A rough one."

"I just had two," the kid said defensively.

"Why the hell did you stay in, then? I had to have aces to open." I didn't mention that he'd raised me: why rub it in?

"I didn't think you had them," he said, and shuffled.

So he was calling me a liar. Big fucking deal. But I found myself wondering, back in the back of my head someplace, why a house dealer would be playing so stupid, and why a guy working for the house would be carrying desperation around in his watery eyes.'

Then again, my eyes were watery, too, and I wasn't desperate. I was just reacting to the layer of smoke created by all the gamblers in the room whose penchant for games of chance extended to lung cancer roulette.

I stayed a few more hands, not wanting to leave the table at a point where doing so might cause a scene, and came away with three hundred and eighty-some bucks, and that didn't include what I spent on the four or five Cokes I drank while at the table.

In spite of which, I was still thirsty, and I went over to the bar area, which was the least busy part of the room, except for the trio of waitresses hustling back and forth with trays of booze for the members at the gaming tables.

In fact, when I crawled up on a padded stool at the bar, I was alone. Except for the bartender, or rather barmaid, whose shapely back was to me at the moment, though I didn't have much doubt the front would be just as nice. Another in the parade of beautiful female employees here at the Barn.

She was on the tall side, with shoulder-length dark blond

hair, and she turned and gave me a wide, earthy smile and said, "What's your pleasure?"

I laughed.

Now that wasn't the most original line I ever heard, nor the wittiest, but I laughed.

It was a nervous laugh, a laugh to cover any of the surprise that might have shown through when I found out who she was.

For one thing, she had a name tag on her red sweater that said "Lucille," meaning she was the pleasant voice on the telephone who had directed me here.

For another thing, she was Glenna Cole.

9

SHE DIDN'T RECOGNIZE ME.

At least I didn't think she did. Nothing showed in her eyes, or anywhere else. Maybe I'd managed to watch her all that while back in Florida without her noticing, after all. Maybe my trick of shaving off the beard had worked. Maybe my efforts to complete my half-face tan had been worth the bother.

Or maybe she was just better than me. Maybe she could be surprised without registering it one iota. Maybe she could recognize somebody without having to cover with a silly nervous laugh. Maybe a lot of things.

Right now she was waiting.

And it took me a beat to remember what it was she was waiting for, which was the answer to the musical question, "What's your pleasure?"

"Coke," I said.

"Don't tell me you're the guy," she said.

I managed not to do my famous nervous laugh this time.

"What guy?" I said.

"The guy who's been ordering the straight Cokes all night long. Don't you know that stuff's not good for you?"

I'd said Coke only to be saying something. Simple reflex. Truth was, all that caffeine-loaded cola had helped make me feel jumpy, and left me with a lousy taste in my mouth as a bonus.

But it was an opening, a place to start a conversation, so I followed up.

"I suppose booze'd be better for me?"

"Sure. Ever see what a nail looks like when you leave it in Coke over night?"

"Can't say as I have."

"Eats the sucker up. Like acid."

"You convinced me."

"You're swearing off Coke."

"No. But I won't go leaving nails in it."

She laughed, just a little. Not a nervous one, either. Not covering up anything. I didn't think.

"Somehow you don't seem the type," I said.

"Which type is that?"

"Bartender type."

"Is that it? You don't trust lady bartenders?"

"Can you make a gimlet?"

"Can I make a gimlet? Gin or vodka?"

"Gin. Make yourself something, too."

She went away and made a gin gimlet for me and something for herself and I sat wondering how I could ever have failed to recognize that voice on the phone earlier today. Sometimes the full timbre of a voice is lost over the wires. On the phone hers had seemed pleasant, sultry, but that's all. Here, now, in person, I was reminded of how haunting that baritone but in no way masculine voice of hers had seemed to me when I was first hearing it, memorizing it, learning to pick it out from the giggly crowd down round the pool at the Beach Shore. It was a voice I should have recognized, even though tonight was my first conversation with her.

She brought me the gimlet and I sipped it and nodded approval.

She sipped the Manhattan she'd made herself and said, "I know you from someplace."

Well, now.

"Shouldn't that be my line?" I said.

She gave me that earthy smile again, the gums showing, but attractive as hell. "Maybe so. You a regular here?"

"No. I'm from out of town. Why? Are you new?"

"New? Not exactly. This is my first night on the job at the Barn, if that's what you mean. But new I'm definitely not. Hey, I do know you from someplace. Really. "

"I talked to you on the phone this afternoon."

"Oh, yes! I gave you directions."

"Pretty damn good ones, too, for a first-nighter."

"Well. I just got here this morning myself, came by way of Des Moines like you did, so it was all pretty fresh in my mind."

A waitress with short blond hair, an attractive pout, and perky little breasts that poked at her barn red sweater came up alongside me and said to Lucille (as Glenna Cole was calling herself here), "I hate to bust up this budding romance, but I got a couple dozen booze-happy cardplayers who'd be happy to get the couple dozen drinks you're supposed to be making."

"I'll get right on it," Lucille said. But those oriental eyes said Go fuck yourself.

Which didn't in the least bother the pouty blond waitress, who parked herself on the stool next to me while the drinks were getting made.

"You got a smoke?" she said.

"No," I said.

"I'll do you a favor sometime," she said, and moved over a stool.

I nursed my gimlet.

"Hey," I said, after a while.

The pouty blonde, not looking, said, "You talking to me?"

"Yeah. Tell me something."

"Such as."

"Who's that big guy that's been circulating all evening?"

A guy about fifty, a young-looking and healthy fifty at that, several inches over six foot, short-cropped white hair, modest pot belly, craggy good looks, had been winding through the tables incessantly as long as I'd been there, though he never would butt in, never made conversation unless a player at a table began it, a constant presence in the room without being obnoxious about it. And though he wore a conservative but well-tailored suit with a solid-color blue tie, he had a rugged look that fit right in with the image the Barn sought.

"Why don't you take a great big guess and see if you just can't figure it out yourself?"

"He runs the place."

"He owns it, too."

"What's his name?"

"Tree."

"What?"

"Tree, I said. Frank Tree."

"Is that a real name?"

"How should I know? Ask Mr. Tree."

"You still want a smoke?"

"Sure."

I got a buck out and wadded it up and tossed it down the counter in front of her.

"Buy yourself a couple packs," I said.

She turned her nose up at the wadded-up buck. Then she put it in her denims.

Meanwhile, Lucille was on her way back with a tray full of drinks. One of the drinks was another gimlet for me; the rest of the tray went with the pouty waitress out into the room of cardtables.

I tasted the fresh drink and said, "I may give up Coke completely."

"Oh shit," Lucille said. "Here comes another empty tray to fill. Listen. We close in an hour and a half. I'll be out of here fifteen minutes after that. Let's do something."

"Fine," I said.

While I was waiting I went back out to the tables. By closing I'd lost half of my winnings from draw poker at seven-card stud.

I wasn't sure yet whether I was winning or losing tonight.

10

―――――――――――――――――――――――

―――――――――――――――――――――――

"*YOU'LL HAVE TO* excuse this place," she said, flicking on the light as we came in and locking the door behind us, "but I haven't exactly had much time for decorating. As a matter of fact I haven't unpacked."

"Looks fine to me," I said.

It also looked small: one twelve-by-twelve room serving as living room and bedroom and everything else, except for a cubbyhole kitchenette off to the far right and a bathroom to the near right. There was a beat-up couch against the left wall, a coffee table nearby, an armchair by the window, and on the kitchen table a portable television with a screen the size of a *TV Guide* folded in half. The walls were plaster, light green, the carpet wall to wall but worn, dark green. Not an elegant layout, but clean and not as depressing as some places I been in. The major problem was a pygmy could get stir crazy in there.

"I'll fix us something to drink," she said.

"Nothing with booze."

"This time I agree with you. Instant Sanka okay?"

"Sounds fine."

"Just take a second to make. You go ahead and pull out the bed."

"The bed."

"You know, the couch. It's a hideaway bed."

"Oh. Well, sure."

I pulled out the bed.

"Are there sheets on it?" she asked from the kitchenette.

"Yeah. Also some blankets."

"That's a relief. This friend of mine who was supposed to be getting this apartment ready for me, well, she's a kind of a scatterbrain. I didn't expect things to be so well organized. She's got the cupboard and refrigerator stocked for me and everything."

"How's the Sanka coming?"

"Just take a minute to get the water heated up. Go ahead and make yourself comfortable."

"On the bed, you mean."

"Of course on the bed. Is it hot in here?"

"A little, yes."

"I don't think the heat can be turned down. I think the thermostat's broken or something."

She fixed the Sanka, brought a cup over to me, and pulled off the sleeveless red sweater she'd filled out so admirably at the Barn. "I hope you know I'm taking terrible advantage of you."

"Oh?"

"Sure," she said, undoing her bra. "If it wasn't for you I

would've had to hitch a ride home with one of those creeps at the Barn. And you saw how well I got along with the waitresses there."

"Maybe they were just giving you a hard time because it's your first day."

"First day and every day. I mean, I make more money than they do, so what can you expect? I could've got a ride from one of those guys dealing for the house, I suppose, but fraternizing with them is against policy, I'm told. Besides, I didn't see anything in that room that appealed to me . . . with one exception." She unzipped her denims. "Excuse me a second, would you?" She let the denims drop, stepped out of them and went into the bathroom.

"You see, I have a car of my own," she called over some running water, "but I loaned it to my girl friend."

"The one who got this apartment for you?"

"That's right. How could I refuse her? She gave me a ride out there and I told her I could find a ride back. And I did, didn't I?"

She emerged from the bathroom, walked over to the kitchenette, got her own cup of Sanka, and flicked off the kitchen light, and the overhead light, too. She was wearing transparent panties. That's all. She'd left a light on in the bathroom, and left the door open a crack, but otherwise it was dark in there. Still, I could see just fine. Subdued lighting can do nice things to a naked body. Nearly naked.

She was a study in dark and light contrast: dark Florida tan against the untanned flesh where her bikini had been, dark nipples against otherwise white breasts, dark pubic bush against the whiteness of her loins.

She was an architectural wonder, this girl. One day, if she lived long enough, those massive breasts would have to droop. Gravity, like death, is inevitable. But right now she and her high, huge breasts were alive and well in Des Moines, Iowa.

"Sorry I was such bad company, on the way here," she said, stretching out on her stomach on the bed, cupping her chin with one long-nailed hand, the dark blue, gold-flecked eyes with their oriental slant catching what little light there was and making electricity out of it.

"Bad company?"

"Yes. I'm afraid I slept all the way."

And she had, head against my shoulder, for the whole thirty-minute ride from the Barn to the east side of Des Moines where this apartment was.

"You didn't snore," I said.

"I never snore."

"Neither do I."

"I want you to know something."

"Okay. What is it?"

"I don't usually do this kind of thing. I want you to know that."

"Do what kind of thing?"

"You know. Fuck on the first date."

"How do you know we're going to?"

"Just a hunch."

"You may be right. But right now I'm going to drink this Sanka."

"See."

"See what?"

"You do think I do this kind of thing all the time."

"If I said something, I'm sorry."

"You didn't say anything. It was how you said it."

"I'll pretend I understand that. I'm done with my Sanka."

"Well, I'm just starting mine."

"I'll wait."

"What the fuck's your name, anyway?"

"Jack."

"You already know my name."

"Lucille. Lucy?"

"Lucille."

"Lucille, then. How'd you get in the bartending business, Lucille?"

"I had a husband who owned a nightclub in Detroit. He thought it was good psychology to have a good-looking woman tending bar. Also it was cheaper, since he was married to me and didn't have to pay me."

"Had a husband?"

"That's right."

"Divorced?"

"No. They killed him."

"They?"

"Some mob people."

"No kidding?"

"Yeah. They were his silent partners and he was screwing them. They warned him and he didn't listen. It was his fault, really."

"You have a pretty cool attitude about it."

"Not cool. Cold. I loved the little prick in the beginning. He was older than me, I was just a waitress in his place, impressed by the boss making advances. He had a wife at the time, who he dumped for me. He was really a little prick. But I was impressionable. Didn't finish high school, that sort of thing. Never had anything going for me but my looks. So much for me. How about you?"

"Well. I could tell you about the time I came home from Vietnam and found my wife in bed with a guy. Or we could forget about the sad stories and fuck."

"Good idea," she said.

11

SHE WAS GONE when I woke up. On the coffee table was a note: "Jack—you looked too restful to wake. Had a hair appointment and some other errands. Orange juice in the fridge. If you're still in town, stop at the Barn tonight. If you want. L."

I had a shower and got dressed, had some orange juice, and looked around the place a little.

But carefully. I didn't pick anything up or look inside anything. Don't think it wasn't a temptation to get in that suitcase over in the corner, or to go through the double-door closet or through the drawers of the tiny dresser in the bathroom.

There are ways to tell if somebody's been through your things. Traps you can lay before going out. You can apply a faint layer of baby powder to the inside of a drawer, for instance, or lay a thread or hair or something across the joining of two closet doors, or balance a little piece of metal or plastic or anything on the snap of a suitcase. There are a lot of tricks like that. I don't know them all, and don't bother with any myself, but a lot of people do.

Why else would she leave me here alone, if not to test me? Wasn't that why she'd picked me up last night? She'd made the move, after all, not me. I figured she'd recognized me but hadn't been able to place me. I was just a familiar face, but in the business she was in, a familiar face can be big trouble. So she was checking me out. I've been checked out worse ways.

That had to be it. No other way made sense. Women don't usually go crawling in my lap looking for the zipper; not on first sight they don't. Especially not an exotic-looking looker like Lucille or Ivy or Glenna Cole or whoever the hell she was. She sure wasn't the dragon lady, not in the sack anyway.

Oh, she was nice in bed. Better than nice. A slow, hip-grinding, sensual screw that wasn't the whambam of a casual bar pick-me-up, or a phony I-love-you-I-love-you bout like the married ladies indulge in, when they're screwing somebody besides who they're married to.

But she was not exotic. The promise of the oriental eyes was not delivered. It was that earthy, gums-showing smile that kept its word, and that, as I sat at her kitchen table drinking a second glass of orange juice, was what was bothering me, now that I thought about it.

Because she wasn't supposed to be real. She was acting, she had to be, but Christ did she seem real, opening her legs for me, sucking me in, hugging my back, goddamn it was real, nothing fake in it at all, not that I could see anyway, not the joyless copulation of the stag film actress, or the frantic humping of a hooker trying to fool and please at the same time, but something else, something she was caught up in, or seemed to be, and I got caught up in it myself, caught up in her should I say, and it disturbed me. I was supposed to be here to watch her, to see what she was up to and maybe kill her. Not fuck her. And certainly not fuck her and like it.

So I looked around the place without touching anything. There wasn't much to see. The only interesting thing I found was on the window sill. The bottom of the sill was lined with dust. Two round circles were evident in the dust, as if left by two drinking glasses that had been set side by side, making their mark.

But it wasn't drinking glasses that had made the mark. It was another sort of glasses. Binoculars.

I parted the curtains, looked out the window. I saw the parking lot, where I'd left my GT last night; beyond that a quiet side street, on the other side of which was an obviously high-rent apartment house.

Lucille's apartment was on the third floor of a three-story building in a sleazy little block in a sleazy little area known as the East Side. To be fair, not every place of business on the East Side fell into that category. For every three or four Nude Go Go Bars there was a plumbing supply outfit or an auto parts shop or the like; there was even a bank and a drug store or two, left over from when the East Side had been the hub of the city, and not its most embarrassing eyesore, a ragtag collection of junk shops, porno houses and seedy bars, crouching at the foot of the gold-domed, archaically ornate Capitol Building like a poor relation waiting for the reading of the will.

Like the Capitol Building, the high-rent apartment house

sat on one of a series of bluffs that rose above the deteriorating East Side, and the rest of the city too, for that matter. Unlike the Capitol Building, the apartment house was modern in style, a curved slab of white brick and black glass. Alone on its hill, aloof, it was bordered by a neighborhood of factories at the hill's foot, and churches, clinics, government buildings and more apartment complexes at its rear.

A drive curving up the slope was clearly marked private. The place was undoubtedly well guarded, and even without the use of the binoculars I knew were somewhere in this apartment, I could see a pair of uniformed private cops on duty in the spacious parking lot that surrounded the building like a moat. The people living there probably felt pretty safe. Most of them probably were. One of them wasn't.

One of them was being watched from this window by the woman currently calling herself Lucille Something. I thought I knew who it was she was watching, and I'd spend the rest of the day confirming that suspicion, and then I'd be in business.

Unless she killed the poor son of a bitch before I had a chance to do something about it.

12

SATURDAY NIGHT, ABOUT midnight, Frank Tree got in his LTD and by the time he was settled behind the wheel, leaning forward to insert key in ignition, I had put the fat cold nose of the silenced nine-millimeter up against the side of his neck, just under his ear.

I had to give the guy credit. He didn't jump. Hell, he didn't flinch. He didn't yell, either. And he knew enough not to turn towards me. He didn't try looking at the rear-view mirror, as if he knew in advance I'd turned it to face the windshield.

All he did was say: "I don't have any money on me."

"Good. I'm glad to hear you're not a total idiot."

"What?"

"Didn't you ever hear of locking your car? How many hundred buck tape decks do you lose a week?"

"What is this?"

I leaned back a little, eased the gun off his neck. "Look on the seat next to you," I said. "Tell me what you see. "

"A shirt."

"Tell me about it."

"It's pale lemon color. It's got a monogram on the pocket. It's dirty."

"What else."

"It's mine."

"Where do you suppose I got it?"

"My dirty laundry, I guess. So you've been in my apartment. So what?"

"So now I'm in your car and I got a gun on you."

"Yeah,, well, congratulations. Now what the fuck's this all about?"

"It's about a guy who drives an LTD and makes a hell of a lot of money, who leaves his car unlocked and lives in an apartment you can open with a credit card, in an apartment building whose security is a joke."

"There are two armed guards on duty twenty-four hours a day at Town Crest."

That was the name of the high-rent apartment building I could see from Lucille's window. Frank Tree was a tenant.

"Those guys aren't guards," I said. "They're parking lot attendants. Anybody in a jacket and tie can walk in the lobby and go up the elevator and nobody says a word."

"Is there a point to this?"

"The point is if I'd been hired to kill you, you'd be dead by now."

"Hired to . . ."

"The only problem I can see in killing you is trying to pick from the dozens of ways to do it. I heard of sitting ducks, but this is ridiculous."

Tree brought a hand up, and I touched the back of his neck with the silenced gun. But he was only scratching his head. A few flakes of dandruff floated onto his shoulders.

"I can offer you double," Tree said. "Double whatever you're being paid."

"You don't understand. No one's paying me. Yet. I only said *if* I'd been hired to kill you."

"What is this, some kind of extortion racket? Maybe you don't know the kind of people I count as friends."

"Mafia guys, you mean? They probably helped get you into this."

"Into what?"

"You're being watched. You're being set up."

"Watched? Set up for what?"

"What do you think?"

"Hey, I don't have an enemy in the world."

"Sure. Hitler probably felt the same way. Anyway, I've already established you're going to be killed."

"Established . . . ?"

"You got two weeks, at the outside."

"Two weeks . . ."

"I'll be going now. Don't turn around as I go."

"But . . ."

"I'll call you tomorrow, Frank. Sleep well."

13

THE STAIRWELL WAS dark. An hour ago I'd been in the back seat of Tree's car in the Barn parking lot. I was preoccupied, wondering how tomorrow would go. This crucial first meeting with Tree had gone well enough, but that was the easy part: scaring him. Tomorrow I had to reason with him, which was where it could get hard.

I was alone. She'd given me the key to her apartment and told me to go on ahead. She had her own car tonight, so why didn't I take off a little early and get the frozen pizza in the oven and put the hot water on for Sanka, and go ahead and get started on the late show, if my eyes were up to the postage stamp screen of her portable. She'd be along soon.

The stairs creaked; the walls of the stairwell were peeling paint; the smell of disinfectant hung heavy. Light seeping out around the doors on either side of the little platform of a second-floor landing made me feel less alone, but the third-floor landing was long, more a hallway, though there were only two apartments up here, one of which was empty. Or anyway she'd told me it was empty. I noticed light along the bottom crack of the door and wondered if somebody had just moved in today or what.

And I had this prickly feeling, on the back of my neck, that made me wish I still had the silenced nine-millimeter on me, and I swung my arm back and gave the guy coming up behind me, from out of the shadows of the landing over to my right, an elbow in the face. Felt like I caught a cheek, flesh and then sharp bone, but it was dark and an elbow isn't the most sensitive part of the body to be making such distinctions with, so who knows.

The important thing was I'd sensed the guy in time, and I was drawing back my right foot to kick his balls up inside him when that apartment door opened, flooding the landing with light, and somebody hit me with something.

14

I FELT MY face moving. Back and forth. Then I heard a clapping sound. Face moving, clapping sound, like I was clapping with my face, and I came out of it chuckling, laughing at how silly it was, clapping with your face, and opened my eyes and looked into bright light, and the guy stopped slapping me.

I never saw his face. I saw nothing but the light. A lamp I guess it was, with a hundred watt bulb or maybe something stronger. Anyway all I saw was light, and the guy, who was somewhere behind the light, right behind it, said, "What's your name?"

"Jack Wilson."

That was the name I was registered under at the Holiday Inn. The phony driver's license in my wallet had it, too.

"What are you doing here?"

"Going blind."

"You know, I can jam this .38 up your ass and see how you like it."

The light was blinding me, all right, but I didn't have to see to know I didn't want a .38 jammed up my ass.

"I'll ask again," he said. "What are you doing in Des Moines?"

"Looking for work."

"What kind?"

"Any kind. Salesman."

"What are you doing hanging around the Barn?"

"Playing some cards. Banging the lady bartender."

"It's time you moved on."

"Anything you say."

And he put out the light.

He hit me with it.

15

MY EYES PEELED slowly open and she was right in on top of me, leaning over me, fingers plucking at my face, her oriental eyes narrowed like I was something interesting to look at.

"What are you doing?" I said.

"Picking glass out of your face," she said.

"Oh."

"You're not too badly cut. Lot of little nicks is about all, really. But we better get this glass out."

"Be my guest."

"Ouch!"

"What?"

"Little fucker nicked me." She held a half-inch sliver of glass up by a thumb and forefinger for me to see. When I had, she dropped the sliver, sucked the forefinger a second.

I sat up on the couch. "How'd you get me back in your apartment?"

"I walked you over here."

"You mean dragged me? I was unconscious, wasn't I?"

"Not entirely. More like drunk."

"I think somebody hit me with a lamp."

"I think so, too. Anyway there's a busted bulb all over the floor next door. All but the pieces of it I been picking out of your face, that is."

"That's where you found me?"

"The door was open, you were on the floor, against the wall, glass all over your face. I thought you were dead for a minute."

"No such luck. Who's your new neighbor? The guy that wrote *Psycho*?"

"Nobody lives next door. Not that I know of."

"Help me off this couch. I want to go see for myself."

She did.

The door was still ajar. I went in carefully, reaching a hand around to switch on the light before going in all the way.

And saw an apartment exactly like Lucille's, with one exception: it was unfurnished.

Some shattered, bloody glass lay near one wall; so did the screw-in socket of the bulb with its claw of red-flecked glass shards sticking out.

"Let's go back," she said, a hand on my shoulder.

"Let's."

She locked the door and nightlatched it. A lot of doors in the Midwest don't have nightlatches. I was glad hers did, though I had no reason to feel safer locked in here with her than I'd been next door with the guy who'd used my face to switch off the lights.

Did I say "guy"? No. There were two of them: the one who came up behind me; and the one who opened the door. Of course the one who opened the door could've been a woman.

"Listen, I think there's some mercurochrome in the bathroom cabinet. You better let me dab some on."

"Go ahead."

She went and got the stuff, and I had a sip of the Sanka she'd found time to make.

"This'll hurt," she said, and began daubing it on.

It did hurt. I felt a tear roll down my cheek and she made a concerned face and with her free hand brushed the tear away. Then she put little bandaids over each cut. Pressed them gently into place.

When she touched my face like that, it bothered me. When she looked at me concerned like that, it bothered me. The way she'd been in bed the other night bothered me, too. Responsive. Giving. Loving.

The bitch was a killer. More importantly, so was I. How could she seem so genuine? Why did she strike a chord in me, even when I knew she had to be faking?

This was only the second night I'd been with her.

I'd left her apartment Friday morning before she got back, and spent the afternoon watching her window from the parking lot below. I was at an angle she couldn't easily spot, and I was sitting in a car she wouldn't recognize as mine, a Ford I rented for the occasion. I didn't need a particularly good vantage point. A good look wasn't what I was after. I just wanted to see the glimmer of circular glass. I just wanted to see the binoculars at the window. And I saw them, all right.

And I saw Frank Tree drive down the curved lane of the Town Crest apartment building around four-thirty in the afternoon, and the reflecting binoculars disappeared in the window, and I pulled the Ford around the block to watch her come down from her apartment, out the door by the rundown storefront, get in her Corvette across the street at the curb, and take off.

I hadn't been surprised. I'd spotted her watching Tree that first night at the Barn, and figured she wasn't watching him because she had the hots for him, either, though he was handsome enough. I knew even then he was her target, but I needed more.

Friday night I got it. She was watching him even closer now, didn't miss a move he made. What she was doing wouldn't begin to show to the casual observer, but I've done that kind of watching myself, and had no trouble picking up on it. In fact I was watching her that way; I could risk it, since she knew I had the hots for her.

She had begged off that night, saying she had promised that girl friend of hers they'd get together for a drink at one of their apartments, after the Barn closed, and I'd be bored silly by all that girl talk anyway, so . . .

So I complied. It was fine with me. I was planning to beg off myself. I had other things to do.

Such as keep watching her. I still had that rental Ford, and followed her from the Barn to a place on University in Des Moines, not far from the Holiday Inn where I was staying. It was a dinner theater, a big brick two-story building with a block of parking lot and a billboard of a sign saying Candle Lite Playhouse, with the name of the current production (*Born Yesterday*) beneath. The parking lot was nearly empty; one of the handful of cars was Tree's LTD. Soon Tree could be seen coming out of the theater in the company of a stacked little blonde in work clothes, who kissed his cheek and scurried back in the building, while Tree reluctantly headed for his LTD and drove to the Town Crest.

Today, in the morning, I repeated my parking lot vigil, but only long enough to determine those binoculars were still poised in her window; and then I drove back to the car rental people and let them have their Ford back.

"You want to tell me about it?" she said.

"About what?"

"About what. About what happened to you. About the fucking glass I picked out of your face."

"Somebody hit me with a lamp. And before that they hit me with something else. Feel the top of my head if you don't believe me."

"That's some goose egg you got there, pardner."

"You're telling me. Got any aspirin?"

"Yeah. But I also got better than that."

And she sat in my lap and put her tongue in my mouth.

"They always tell you to take two," I said.

"Sometimes three."

And we necked for a while, and she said, "So tell me."

"I came upstairs and it was dark on the landing and a guy jumped me. When I came to they shined light in my face and hit me with the lamp. They asked me some questions, too, I think."

"They?"

"Two of 'em. I only heard one talk, though."

"Any idea who they were?"

"No."

"Any idea why they did it?"

"No."

"Your wallet's empty. Maybe that's why."

"Yeah. Could be. I been winning at the Barn."

"How much?"

"Couple hundred a night, on the average."

"Three nights. Six hundred bucks. Where'd you have it?"

"In the wallet."

"All of it."

"All of it."

"You're not the smartest guy I ever met."

"Really? Name somebody smarter."

"The retarded kid in the plumbing joint downstairs."

"Name another."

"You got me. Hey. Who are you, anyway, Jack?"

"Nobody. I used to be a salesman. I'm unemployed right now."

"What did you used to sell?"

"Ladies underwear. The bottom fell out of the bra market."

"Aren't you good at anything but selling underwear?"

"Good at cards."

"You aren't trying to land a seat at the Barn, are you?"

"I don't know. You think maybe I should hit that guy Tree for one?"

There wasn't a flicker of anything in those almond eyes of hers. *You think maybe I should hit that guy Tree* . . . but not a flicker. Christ this bitch was good.

"I'll put a word in for you. I'm new on the job, but I got some pull just the same."

"Oh yeah?"

"Couldn't've got that job if I didn't. Got to have connections in this world, to get by."

"No shit?"

"None. So what do you think? This thing tonight was just a glorified mugging or what?"

"Who knows. You wouldn't happen to have any old boyfriends or anything, would you? Who might be crazy enough to follow you from wherever you came from and beat up your new boyfriends?"

"I hardly think so. It's a long drive from Florida."

Damn! She was telling me too much. The other night she'd told me the story about mob people killing her husband, and I knew, from reading her file, that the story was true. And her name, her goddamn real name, it *was* Lucille. I'd have felt a lot better if she'd lie to me more.

What was she doing, anyway, baiting me? She asks me what happened, how was it I happened to get the piss beat out of me just now, when she was probably there when I was getting that lamp busted across my face. She was playing me like a kazoo.

"Let's fold the couch out," she said.

"I'm too weak. You'll have to do it."

"Pull out the bed you mean? Or the rest, too?"

"Just the bed. On the other, if you want to start without me, go ahead. I'll catch up."

She laughed a little, like she meant it. I laughed, too. Like I meant it. The fuck of it is I did mean it. That's what bothered me.

Then she turned the couch into a bed and we used it.

16

SHE SAID SHE didn't snore, and she didn't, but she was sleeping deep just the same, that fine, full chest of hers rising slow and steady and, well, it was with not a little reluctance that I crawled out of bed and got in my clothes and left her.

My GT was in the parking lot below her window. I had a spare sportsjacket stowed under some stuff behind the driver's seat and I took the jacket and shook it and got some of the wrinkles out and put it on. From the glove compartment I took a pair of glasses and my silenced nine-millimeter. I put the glasses on and stuck the gun in my belt and glanced up at her window. Dark. Curtains still drawn, as best I could tell. The change of jacket and the glasses were for her benefit, should she wake up and get back to doing her stakeout number, in which case she could conceivably see me going in or out of the Town Crest, and in that event the jacket and glasses and distance would hopefully keep her from recognizing me.

The jacket and a tie were all it took to get into the Town Crest, even at three in the morning. That and the twenty I handed the guard in the front lot, when I asked him to park the GT for me. I had him put it in the back lot, which was unlit and presented less of a chance of being spotted by somebody with binoculars across the way.

The modern exterior of the Town Crest was more than matched in its cold sterility by the interior, which looked to have been designed by a mortician who read science fiction. The walls were smooth and white, like eggshells pressed flat. Diffused light glowed down from the white tile ceiling, some of it swallowed up by the black carpet. The elevators were shiny metal that reflected like a compassionate mirror. I pushed the UP button and turned away from my soft-focus reflection while I waited.

Tree's room was on the top floor, the twelfth, down a wide white hail to the right and at the end. I opened his door with a credit card and went in. No lights were on, but I was familiar with the place from my previous visit, in the afternoon, and walked quickly across the tufted shag carpet, though I nearly neglected to sidestep the glass-and-plastic coffee table by the half-circle couch on the edge of the spacious living room, just off of which was his bedroom, where I was headed.

His bed was making noise.

Glugg glugg glugg. Like a hundred midgets swallowing,

Then I remembered. It was a waterbed. Red satin sheets, brown leather padded frame. There's nothing more pathetic than a middle-aged man who's trying to be twenty.

He was alone in the thing. Or on it. I don't think you can be "in" a waterbed. Personally I like to be in control of what I'm sleeping in. On.

He was sound asleep.

I put the nose of the silenced gun against his throat.

He woke up.

Sat up, and the bed rolled and rocked under him.

"Don't turn on the lights," I said.

"All right," Tree said. Calmly. The sea beneath wasn't calming yet, though.

"Did you sic some boys on me?"

"I don't even know who the hell you are."

"You know me. You don't know my name, but you know me."

"I don't sic anybody on you, no."

"Somebody did. I got jumped by a couple of guys tonight, and if they are yours, just tell me, and I'll leave town right now. I don't believe in hanging around where I'm unpopular."

"Whoever jumped you, they weren't mine."

"I hope not. There's something you better understand. I'm no danger to you. I'm no threat. I'm maybe your salvation."

"You got a funny way of showing it." He was referring to the nine-millimeter, the nose of which was still up against his Adam's apple.

"I'm just being cautious," I said, easing the gun off, but only a hair. "It's what keeps me alive. You could profit by my example. See, somebody's got you set up for the hit. Now. If you want my help, fine. I can try and get between you and the people trying to kill you. I may even be able to find out who hired the job done. But, on the other hand. If you think I'm insane, or a blackmailer, or some kind of con man, or if you simply prefer to handle the situation yourself, or God forbid go to the cops with it, well that's fine, too. You'll get blown away, but that's no skin off my ass. So. Say the word and I'm on my way. It's up to you."

"What's in it for you . . . helping me, I mean."

"Money."

"How much?"

"What's your life worth to you? It'll be cheap at half the price."

The bed was finally settling down, making a lap lap sound, like waves rolling into shore.

"If someone wants me dead," he said, quietly, "I can use all the help I can get."

"That's good sound thinking. Especially since I'm the *only* help you can get."

"You're right about the police, anyway. With my past, and the laws I'm bending right now, I can't go inviting that kind of trouble. What about my lawyer?"

"Talk to nobody. Your lawyer could've hired it done."

"He's the best friend I have in the world!"

"Murders happen because of family and friends. Crime of passion and premeditated alike. Oh, a stranger'll kill you for money, or out of being crazy, or both. But a stranger doesn't hire you dead. Someone you know does."

"Jesus. Where do we go from here?"

"We talk again. With the lights on. What's your schedule the next couple days?"

"Tomorrow, I mean today, Sunday, we're open noon to midnight. Monday we're closed. I always drive to Iowa City on Mondays. To visit my son. He's in the hospital there."

"You go alone?"

"Yes."

"What time Monday do you leave?"

"Around ten. I get there about noon."

"There's a Holiday Inn at the Interstate turn-off at the Amanas. Stop for lunch."

"All right. Anything I should do between now and then?"

"Do you carry a gun?"

"No, but I have one. A .38."

"You can use it?"

"Yes."

"Carry it. And put a nightlatch on your door."

"Done. Anything else?"

"You might try sleeping on the floor. Somebody shoots at you in bed, even if they missed, you could drown. Good night."

17

"DID YOU GET *up* in the middle of the night and go out?"
she asked, at breakfast. "Or was I dreaming?"

Even in the morning she looked good. She'd got up
before me and washed her hair, and was wearing a towel
around her head like a turban. Her face was clean and
unblemished and free of make-up, though still dark with
Florida tan, and she looked young, or anyway as young as
those eyes of would allow.

She was wearing a housewifely patchwork robe that
made her look less than glamorous, but there was no way
known to make her look bad. She looked good.

I was in my underwear. My hair was greasy, my teeth
unbrushed, my face unshaven. I was barely awake. I looked
down at the plate of scrambled eggs. I looked back up and

managed to say, "You weren't dreaming. I did get up. I went out and drove around a couple hours."

"What possessed you to do that?"

"It's something I do sometimes. Just go out and drive. Helps me think."

"About what?"

"In this case, about getting mugged by those guys last night. Wondering if there's anything I can do about it. Any way to find them and get my money back and pay them back a little, too. I suppose I could go to the cops about it . . ."

"Why bother? That six hundred bucks of yours is long gone by now, don't you think?"

"I suppose you're right. I guess my ego was just a little bruised, that's all."

"Are you serious about asking Frank Tree for work?"

"I am if you're serious about putting in a good word for me."

"Sure."

And so I asked her. I couldn't see any reason why not. And I didn't know anybody better to ask. So I did. I asked her, "What do you know about this guy Tree, anyway?"

She gave me a confused little smile for a moment, while she searched my face wondering what I was up to, no doubt.

"I don't know a hell of a lot," she said.

"Whatever it is, it's more than me."

"Well, the Barn is a relatively new thing, I know that much. It hasn't been too long since the law passed in Iowa that makes it even possible for a place like the Barn to openly exist."

"Must be a pretty liberal law. Or is Tree just greasing the right wheels?"

"Little of both, I'd say. The law makes gambling legal in

situations where there's a 'social relationship.' Such as a private club, or any place where the gathering is social, whether it's bingo in the church parlor or poker in the back room of a bar. Certain things are still illegal . . . blackjack, craps, roulette, and there's a fifty-dollar win or loss limit, in a twenty-four hour period. But all of that can be gotten around. Obviously."

"Sounds like your employer knows how."

"He should. I hear he used to have a place in Illinois, on the Mississippi, in some little town that was really wide open. Across from Burlington, Iowa. Anyway, he had a place there, like the Barn, only rougher. No restaurant number, just a casino set-up, and booze, of course. Booze wasn't legal in Iowa on Sundays, so Sunday was a big night for a place like that, people coming across the river to sin in Illinois."

"I wonder why he left."

"The laws got changed. Booze on Sundays is legal in Iowa now, and you know about the gambling law. So he moved back to Des Moines and opened the Barn."

"Back to Des Moines?"

"Yeah, I understand he was involved in some things here in the late '40s and early '50s, but I don't know what. That's all I know about the man. It's just stuff I picked up off my girl friend Ruthy, and the bitches at work. They're all hot for his bod, you know."

"Really. Does he hump the help?"

"Not *this* help, he doesn't. Anyway, he's too good a businessman to do that, I think."

"What's your personal opinion of the guy? What kind of boss is he?"

"Best way to describe him is he's a man's man. He can drink without getting drunk, tell you who won the 1952

World Series, play poker for six hours and get up and pee and sit down and play six more."

"That doesn't say what kind of boss he is."

"Well, he's a pleasant enough boss. Friendly, even. But businesslike, like I said. Fuck up and you're fired."

"I see. Good poker player?"

"Very. Oh, and he hates to see anybody lose, if you buy his act. Truth is, he'd take your last dime. Likes to win all the way, at whatever cost . . . to his opponents, I mean."

"You sound like a pretty good judge of character."

"I'm a bartender, aren't I? Besides, how do you know I'm right? Maybe this is just a bunch of bullshit."

"Because I'm not a bad judge of character myself. Got any more of that Sanka?"

"Sure."

She filled my cup and I said, "What time do you have to be at work?"

"Not till six."

"What time is it now, eleven? Want to take in a movie this afternoon or something?"

"I got a better idea," she said, sitting down, sipping her own cup. "There's a good dinner theater here that has Sunday matinees and a great buffet lunch. Want to give it a try?"

"Wouldn't happen to be that place over on University, would it?"

"Yeah, that's the one."

That was the place where Frank Tree had met with that busty little blond girl friend of his, the other night.

"Why not?" I said. "I can appreciate good acting."

18

THE CANDLE LITE Playhouse was a modern brick two-story that looked somewhat cold and even austere from without, but within was decorated in warm golds and greens. The plush floral carpet, subdued lighting, piped-in muzak and cozy tables conspired to make the large room seem intimate. We were seated at the edge of the balcony, at a table barely big enough to hold its glass-enclosed candle (as yet unlit, by the way), and sipped a drink before going down to the stage, where the food was being served, the set and its props having been scooted back to accommodate a generous buffet. It looked a little odd, people parading up the few steps onto the stage, going through the cafeteria line collecting their food, then exiting nervously, awkwardly, balancing the several filled plates, coming off the stage like bit players who had wandered into the wrong scene. The stage, Lucille explained, had been the altar of the place when it had been a church.

"Church?"

"Yeah," she said. "Some crazy evangelist type thing. They had a young guy who thought he was the Second Coming or something. Or at least the second Billy Graham. He had a big following here, even had his own radio show, but he got an offer to do the same thing for more money someplace in Texas, I think, and once he was gone everything just sort of fizzled, church went bankrupt. Some local people got together and bought and remodeled the place into this."

"Either way it's show business," I said. "For somebody new in town, you sure know all the local gossip."

"Ruthy just talks a lot, that's all."

"Ruthy?"

"I've mentioned her before, haven't I? She's the friend who got that apartment lined up for me, before I even got here. She's also the one who got us this good a seat at such short notice. She works here."

"Am I ever going to meet her?"

"You'll see her a little later."

I decided not to pursue that. The way I was playing this allowed me to ask a lot of questions; in fact, pretending ignorance, as I was, required that I ask a lot of questions. But it would be wrong to press, so I waited till our drinks were finished, then rose, pulled out her chair and walked her down a softly carpeted, gently winding stairway to the main floor, where we joined the food line, climbed onto the stage, and came back to our balcony table with our food, which we ate.

As buffets go, it wasn't bad. The salad bar was

unimaginative, just a couple kinds of jello with stuff floating in it, and coleslaw and lettuce salad, apply your own dressing. But the roast beef was rare and tender, and several kinds of potatoes and vegetables and other side dishes made it a very pleasant Sunday dinner.

The company was pleasant, too. She was wearing a dark brown pants suit, perhaps the same one I'd seen her in as she was leaving the Beach Shore, in the middle of the night, not so long ago. If it was, I remember it'd seemed mannish to me, at the time. Perhaps that was because I didn't know the jacket came off to reveal a yellow-and-tan-striped halter top that caressed her large breasts, cradled them like a child sleeping in a hammock.

Somebody came around and lit our candle. It threw shadows on her face, making her features seem even more exotic than usual. She wasn't wearing any make-up on her eyes. She didn't have to.

I was taking a perverse enjoyment in the verbal games we were playing, neither of us aware of what the stakes were, exactly, but both aware we were playing something, maybe nothing more than the sex game, or anyway that was the conclusion I hoped she'd come to, and maybe she had, if I was succeeding at convincing her I really was just a guy who used to sell brassieres.

I knew one thing. I knew I had to be something of a pain in the ass to her, since she was obviously playing the back-up role here, surveilling Tree till her partner (who I assumed was the guy who'd worked me over with the lamp) got ready to make the hit. I was in her way, making it impossible for her to properly keep an eye on Tree, to get his movements, his pattern down; but my presence here was suspicious enough to make it necessary for her to keep track of me, at least until she was sure of who the hell I was or wasn't. Otherwise she'd have to forget the Tree contract entirely; she was a pro, and couldn't operate any other way. She'd beg off the job, tell her middle man to tell their client to get somebody else because this one just didn't smell right to her.

The thing that bothered me was, was she getting to me? And something else bothered me even more: I was starting to entertain the probably stupid notion that *I* might be getting to *her*.

Not to mention this nagging feeling I had that one of us was behaving like an idiot, and I was afraid I knew which one of us it was.

Unless it was both of us . . .

We had another drink, and I decided to move another chess piece.

"There's something I'm having trouble with," I said.

"What's that?"

"Your name. Lucille. It's a nice name. I like it. But I'm having a little trouble using it. It's, I don't know, too formal or something. And you don't look like a Lucy to me. Do people call you Lucy?"

"My folks did. I always hated it."

"So what *do* people call you?"

"Do I have a nickname, you mean? Well. I knew a man who called me Ivy. He seemed to like that name for me."

Ivy. The Broker's name for her. I make a tentative little move, just nudge a pawn out for a look around, and she comes down on me with her fucking queen.

"Ivy," I said. "I don't think it fits you."

"My friends in high school called me Lu. Nobody's called me that in years though."

"Lu." I lifted my gimlet. "Here's to you. Lu."

"Didn't anyone ever tell you not to have so many drinks so early in the day? I'm a bartender. I know."

"Are you going to accept the damn toast, or not?"

"All right." She clinked her glass against mine. "Here's to Lu."

The house lights dimmed. We looked down and the stage had been cleared, the set put back in place, and the play was beginning.

And that was when I found out who her friend Ruthy was.

She was the lead. Playing the Judy Holliday role in *Born Yesterday*, which they were doing in '40s dress and trappings, since that's when the play first came out, and because people like nostalgia, I guess. She was no Judy Holliday, but she was blond, and well-built, and not a bad little actress, for Des Moines.

She was also Frank Tree's girl friend.

But then was that so surprising?

After all, Tree himself was sitting at a ringside table. I saw him there when the house lights went up for intermission.

The bitch had brought me along on her goddamn stakeout.

19

SUNDAY EVENING WAS INTERESTING.

I won a hundred some bucks playing draw poker, but that in itself wasn't particularly interesting. What was was the dealer, the kid with the worried expression and closed mouth and glasses, the one who played stupid every time I sat down at his table, which was every night I'd been there.

So winning a few bucks from him was nothing special. In fact I usually won a little bigger.

But it was unusual to see him wearing make-up.

I don't mean to imply he was queer or anything (though you never know). I don't mean he was wearing lipstick or mascara or rouge. It was makeup, flesh-colored stuff, the theatrical-type liquid some women use in place of powder these days. He'd applied it along one cheek, across the cheekbone and down a ways. That side of his face was a little fucked up, a little puffy. The make-up did a fair job of disguising it, and the somewhat dim lighting in the room helped, too. But his face was fucked up, no question, like maybe he'd been in a fight.

Like maybe somebody had given him an elbow in the face.

He didn't say much that night. He didn't say much any night. He let his cards speak for him, and they didn't say much either, except that he was lousy.

I listened to what little he did say, though. You can't play poker and not let out a few words, now and then, especially sitting in the dealer's chair. So I listened and tried to match the voice with the voice behind the light that had shined in my eyes last night.

At one point one of the other players commented casually on the bandages on my face. I still had five of them, covering little cuts I'd got from where the lamp caught me. I gave a small speech about how people who use electric razors shouldn't switch all of a sudden to a straight razor unless they don't mind looking like chopped meat for a couple days. The various players laughed politely at that. Everybody but the dealer. He just shuffled his cards and said to the man at his left, "Cut them."

It was the same voice, all right.

I made a mental appointment with him, and returned to my cards.

The other interesting thing that happened Sunday night was Lu (as I was beginning to feel comfortable calling her) had invited me to move in with her.

"Why keep paying for that bed at the Holiday Inn?" she said. "You haven't been using it."

"Your apartment's pretty small. We're going to be tripping over each other."

"That sounds kind of nice."

It did at that.

So I moved in with her, wondering how she was going to manage to watch Tree with me around, knowing that if anyone could find a way it was Lu.

Glenna.

Ivy.

20

WHEN I GOT there Tree was almost finished with his lunch. He was sitting alone, in a booth, eating a bratwurst sandwich. It was eleven and the lull between breakfast and lunch was just about over; soon the coffee shop would be crowded again, and I wanted to talk to him in private.

I went over and smiled and said, "The swimming pool, when you're done."

Tree looked up and his mouth was full but his china blue eyes were empty. He just nodded, looked down again, picked a pickle off his plate and went right ahead eating.

He was a poker player, all right.

The place was a Holiday Inn, but not a typical one. It was situated on the turn-off for the Amana Colonies, which was where some Amish-type settlers had experimented with a crude communistic life style a hundred years ago or so, and the place had affected a rustic look, not unlike Tree's own Red Barn, though somewhat more authentic. The barnwood walls were decorated with framed photographs of somber, bearded pioneers in heavy dark clothing, their wives in bonnets and drab formless dresses, faces full of hard work and well-earned unhappiness.

Some of the pictures showed children, who hadn't been around long enough to get glum, though the teenagers in the pictures were well on their way. There were also some examples of authentic pioneer clothing, under glass, and some old farm equipment and, in little roped-off alcoves, antique furniture was visible, with modern versions of similar furniture displayed here and there, with tags telling where in the Amanas the stuff could be bought.

There was a comfortable sofa along the wall, across from the glass wall through which the large indoor pool could be seen. I sat and watched a middle-aged lady doing laps, and wished there were some younger female swimmers to watch. A nice looking woman of about twenty-five, dark hair, two-piece yellow suit, was down at the far end making use of the sun lamp. A man about sixty sat directly across from me on the other side of the pool, his bloated belly like a beach ball on his lap, a thick cigar in one hand, martini in the other, features of his face lost in a wealth of wrinkles. The middle-aged lady had two kids, or grandkids, I don't know which. One was a boy about ten, the other a girl about eight. They were apparently trying to drown each other. In the glass I could also see my own vague reflection, and that of the wall behind me, with its several framed tintypes of Amana settlers, and various hanging artifacts, ox yoke, pitchfork, wagon wheel, superimposed on the guests enjoying the Holiday Inn pool. Maybe I would have made something profound out of all that, but then Tree was there, sitting down next to me.

He was wearing a stylish sportsjacket, about the color of cigarette smoke, with a dark blue open-collar shirt and white slacks. He smelled of musk cologne and his short white hair was brushed down flat on his head, a butch that had been made to behave. He had the suspiciously sincere smile and hard cool eyes you find in any self-made man. His business could be used cars or gambling, real estate or women, construction or heroin. Whatever. The look is the same.

"I don't believe I caught your name," he said, not looking at me, except maybe in the reflection on the glass wall.

"Quarry," I said.

"That a last name or a first name?"

"It's just something you can call me."

"All right, Mr. Quarry. Convince me."

"Of what?"

"Of all the danger I'm in."

"You're here, aren't you? Doesn't that mean you're already convinced?"

"Maybe so. Let's say I was convinced when you had a gun on me. What I don't know, yet, is how convincing you are unarmed."

"If that's the way you feel," I said, getting up, "I'll just be running along . . ."

He caught my arm. Brought me back down with a strong grip. "One moment. You're a poker player, Mr. Quarry. I've seen you indulging at the Barn, the last week or so. You know, you might have introduced yourself."

"I'm shy."

"Let me make my point. In playing poker, as you well know, there are bets made, and raises, and more raises, and then finally one player calls and gets to look at the other man's hand, before showing his own. Well, we've played our little games, Mr. Quarry. In the dark. And me, I'm always sitting under the gun, it seems, keep having to check to your pat hand. Well this time I'm calling."

I smiled. That was a rehearsed speech if I ever heard one. I wondered if he'd written it down on paper and memorized it or what. No matter. I had him. He already believed me, was convinced he was set up for a hit. He just needed to make up for the minor humiliations I'd put him through those two times. That is, if any humiliation is minor to an ego like his.

Some tourist types, a couple of near-elderly couples, stopped in front of us and stared at the artifacts on the wall over our heads. People were constantly flowing by, which in a strange sort of way afforded us privacy. The glass wall didn't hold in all of the echoing pool noise, and the lobby was nearby, and so was the bar. Just enough commotion to make us invisible, and to keep our conversation to ourselves.

When the aging tourist types moved on, Tree picked up where he left off.

"Maybe I haven't made myself clear," he said. "I know how this kind of thing works. Hitting people, I mean. I know how much it costs. I know the channels you go through to get it done. I know how many people come in to do the job, and what each one does. I been around, in other words. I know some things that you better know, Mr. Quarry, or you may find out the hard way what getting hit is all about."

"I know all those things, Frank."

"Prove it."

"All right. Ask."

"How much does it cost?"

"That depends."

"On?"

"Whether you hire some asshole in a bar for a hundred bucks or something, or you go for real professionals."

"Real professionals."

"Two thousand up."

"How do I get in touch with them?"

"You don't. There's a middle man, a broker."

"I go to him, then."

"No. He gets fed his clients from mob people."

"So these are mob killings we're talking about."

"Not necessarily. Say some businessman has a problem, a wife, another woman, a competitor, a partner, a problem. Say he has a friend, another businessman, who has links to the mob. He asks his friend to put him in touch with somebody who takes care of problems. That puts the wheels in motion."

"How do you know all this?"

"Maybe I used to kill people for money."

"Is that so?"

"Since you already know all this, maybe you hired me once. Who knows?"

But he wasn't out of questions yet. "How many people involved?"

"Three."

"*Three?*" he said. Like he'd caught me.

"There's somebody to do the stakeout work," I said. "And somebody to pull the trigger."

"You said three."

"Sure. The victim makes three, Frank. That's where you come in."

21

THE PSYCHOPATHIC HOSPITAL at Iowa City was a sprawling one-story brick building on a spacious lawn whose many trees and bushes were apparently tailored to provide a soothing landscape, no matter what the season. Only right now it was no season at all, rather that limbo period between winter and spring, trees gray and skeletal, grass brown as cardboard. Even the few evergreen bushes looked wilted, like a salad that sat out.

We came in separate cars. I had already determined that no one (except me) had followed Tree from Des Moines to the Amana turn-off on Interstate 80. But that didn't mean somebody, knowing Tree's patterns, might not drive to Iowa City by some other route and pick up shadowing him there. So Tree parked along the curb of a half-circle drive designed for outpatient pick-up, where you could legally park for thirty minutes or so; and I left my latest rental Ford in a metered stall down the slope of the hill just beyond the hospital. I spent ten minutes trying to see if anybody was here ahead of us, watching, and there didn't seem to be, but I couldn't be sure: the University Hospital was across the way, with its large parking lot, where somebody could easily be staked out. My main concern was not wanting to be recognized, not wanting to be seen with Tree, particularly by Lu, who might be sitting in a car in that lot watching right now. Maybe the ten minutes between Tree going in and me following would be enough; that and my rental car and feeble disguise, consisting of glasses and a sweater I'd pulled on over my shirt, hopefully affecting the look of a straight-type college kid. The man of a thousand faces.

Inside was a hallway, with a glassed-in office area off to the left, with a pretty young nurse in it, who Tree was unsuccessfully flirting with when I came in. I was identified as a cousin of the patient; evidently only relatives were admitted. Then the nurse told Tree that Dr. Cash wanted a word with him before the visitation, and Tree went down the hall and knocked on a door on the right and it opened and he went in.

I waited downstairs, in a room full of tables and chairs and vending machines. This room, like the corridor I'd been briefly in upstairs, was as coldly institutional as a tax form. Some lunch room. I'd sooner have a sandwich in the morgue. Which didn't stop me from feeding some change to a vending machine that sold me a Coke that was all ice and syrup and I drank it anyway.

After that I wandered in the hall a while. This lower floor was apparently in as much use as the upper one, with rooms labeled various functional things. The ceiling was a maze of exposed electrical wiring and pipes, cheerfully painted over in bland pastel, and would have been enough to make your average fire inspector check in as a permanent guest. The only advantage I could see to having the place set up this way, like a two-story building with the first floor underground, was it cut down on people jumping out of windows.

I'd never been in a nuthouse before and hoped this wouldn't start a trend. But there was somebody here Tree wanted me to see, and I'd decided to go along with him, since it seemed to mean a lot to him . . . but by now I was half expecting Tree to come through a door with a brace of boys in white coats and point his finger at me and say, "That's the one."

We had talked money first. I reminded him that in one of our earlier conversations he'd offered double the price of the contract on him. He reminded me that I'd had a gun on him at the time, which, like trying to get a good-looking woman to do what you want in bed, is a situation where a man will say anything.

And then I told him I didn't want him to double the price, anyway.

I just wanted him to match it.

"What are they paying?" he asked.

"I don't know," I said. "But I can make an educated guess."

"Make it, then."

"Five."

There was a short silence, and then he said, "Five thousand dollars," slowly, shaking his head, smiling a little. "A man likes to think his life's worth more than that."

"It's not your life we're talking about, Frank. Just the opposite."

He wanted to know how I'd be paid, and I told him a thousand up front, which would do little more than cover expenses. The balance would come only after I'd got some results. And it would be paid half in cash, half in check, so I'd have something to pay taxes on and keep the IRS happy. There were some details about how the check was to be handled that I needn't go into here.

And he wanted to know what he'd be getting for his money.

I told him he'd already got quite a lot, and explained how I'd followed a woman named Glenna Cole from Florida to Des Moines, where she had been staking him out for five days, and figured she'd watch him no longer than two weeks total before the other half of the team stepped in to finish the job. I didn't mention that Glenna Cole was his lady bartender at the Barn, Lucille. Or that I had tentatively tagged that house dealer of his with the glasses and sullen manner as the trigger. I didn't want to lay too much on him all at once. Especially when he hadn't come across with any cash yet.

"And you'll stop the hit?" he said.

"I'll stop this attempt. I'll try to."

"Meaning what?"

"Meaning I might fuck up and get shot to shit and you along with me."

"And if you don't fuck up, Quarry?"

"There'll still be somebody out there who wants you dead. Who was willing to pay for it once, and'll be willing to pay for it again."

He thought about that a while.

Then he said, "Are you saying you can find out who bought the contract?"

"Maybe. Can't guarantee it."

"There'd be a bonus in it for you."

"You're goddamn right there would."

"How much do you want?"

"Another five."

"Looks like you get double after all."

"You better hope I do, Frank."

And I asked him what enemies he had, if he could think of anybody who'd pay not to have him around.

"I think I might know," he said, a light going on in the back of his head somewhere. "I think I know."

"Who?"

"I don't know the name, or names I mean. But I know who, generally. There are some people into dope I caused some trouble for."

"That doesn't sound like your bag, Frank."

"It's nothing like you're thinking. It's a situation that's hard to explain. . . . I think you'll understand better if you go along with me to Iowa City. There's someone in the hospital there, the Psychopathic Hospital, that-I want you to meet."

"Who?"

"My son."

22

TREE PUSHED THE button and pretty soon somebody came to unlock the big iron doors from the inside and we went in and the doors were locked behind us.

Then we were in a vestibule that was really just a continuation of the corridor we'd been out waiting in. A television blared against the wall on the right, and on the left people were sitting on a couch and some chairs, and we were in the way.

So we moved on quickly, in the company of the lanky short-haired girl in untucked blouse and blue jeans who had let us in and was apparently a nurse. She had the expression of a disillusioned social worker: compassion slowly curdling to boredom and worse.

Everybody wore street clothes, except the doctors, and I

only saw one of those, briefly. It was an attempt at creating an atmosphere of normalcy, I guess. The large, high-ceilinged room we were now in was another attempt at a normal, even casual environment: couches, coffee tables, easy chairs, lamps, all designed to make you feel right at home. The catch was the furniture seemed to have been picked up at a Salvation Army Store clearance sale, but what the hell. It was better than a snake pit.

Over to one side was a quadrangle of couches where patients lounged, some reading old magazines apparently imported from a doctor's waiting room, one middle-aged lady writing a letter, a kid in his late teens or early twenties with a guitar in his lap that now and again he looked at but did not play, a gray-haired man doing a crossword puzzle, a woman about thirty with dishwater blond hair and a round face sitting watching the rest of them. Over by the windows were some cardtables, one of which was in use, three people playing Scrabble, a man and two women, all in their forties, the man and one woman playing silently, the other woman rattling on about her children.

The expressions on the faces in the room were mostly blank. Or full of happiness that was false, or sadness that was real. But mostly blank. Empty.

"This way," the short-haired girl said, with the enthusiasm of a tour guide in a dog food factory.

She led us down a hallway, past a glassed-in office, past a small cafeteria, and into a dormitory area, doors on either side of the hall open and revealing rooms with six or eight beds each in them. We stopped at the last room on the right.

She squeezed out a smile, like that last bit of toothpaste, and said, "Frank's alone today, Mr. Tree, except for Roger, of course."

She left, and we went in. The overhead light in the room

wasn't on; it was like an overcast day in there. The beds were covered with dark gray blankets, the word PSYCHO in gray stencil letters across the pillowcases. There were desks wedged in between beds, and some other desks huddled together in the middle of the room, old, scarred wooden desks, but every patient had his own, and in a room that slept this many, that could be important.

Sitting at one of them, by a window, was a boy about eighteen, in a robe.

He was a younger version of Tree. The major difference, besides years, was dark, longish hair. And the nose was a little different, smaller, the mother's nose, probably.

It was Frank Tree, Jr., and he turned as we came in, and smiled, and turned back to the window.

I didn't see the big guy, at first, standing over in the far corner like a suit of armor, though looking back I don't know how I could have missed him. Seven feet tall and two or three feet wide. You could've hung a billboard on him. He had on a gray tee-shirt that said IOWA on it and brown slacks and white tennis shoes a family of five could've kept their belongings in.

"Is that Roger?" I asked Tree. Quietly.

"That's Roger," Tree said.

And Roger was currently shuffling over toward us like the Frankenstein monster coming to shake his creator's hand.

Which is exactly what he had in mind: shaking our hands. He shook Tree's first, as he seemed to recognize him, and made a sound that didn't resemble any word I know of. When he shook my hand, he made no sound, not even that of bones breaking. Truth is, while he had a hand like a catcher's mitt, Roger's grip was anything but powerful. Limp is the word.

But limp or not, he held on, longer than any sane handshake should, and I had to pull free, grinning back at him as I did, my grin every bit as mindless and shit-eating as his, not wanting to make an enemy of anybody seven feet tall, even if he did shake hands like a dress designer.

"Roger," Tree said, very friendly, "I'd like to talk to Frank Jr. alone now, please."

Roger thought about that a while. He narrowed his eyes, which were wide-set and an eerily beautiful shade of green, in a face with otherwise large, irregular features that seemed to have exploded into being, like a kernel of popped corn. Despite that, it was a young face. Roger couldn't have been older than twenty.

And right now he was pointing a thick finger at me, and looking at Tree, puzzled, saying, "Ah low?"

Alone.

"This is a friend of mine," Tree said. "I'd like him to stay and talk to Frank Jr. with me."

And Roger nodded his head, his shaggy black hair flapping like a cheap wig, and shambled off.

"Retarded, of course," Tree explained.

"I didn't think this place was designed for that kind of thing."

"He's a special case. He gets violent."

"Terrific."

"They have him sedated, now. He's gentle as a kitten."

"Yeah, but does he know that?"

"There's one person he'd never hurt, in any circumstance, and that's Frank Jr. It's pathetic, really, the way he's taken to Frank."

I'd almost forgotten about Frank Jr., who was still sitting silently at the desk, staring out the window.

"Roger is Frank Jr.'s protector," Tree said, in a tone that

mixed melancholy and irony. "Doesn't let Frank out of his sight. Always stands nearby, watching him, guarding him."

"Why?"

"I don't know. I've asked Dr. Cash and he doesn't understand it, either. Maybe it has something to do with Roger feeling sorry for Frank Jr."

That didn't make much sense to me, but I didn't ask him to explain. I was getting uneasy, talking about Frank Jr. like somebody who wasn't around. The fucker was a few feet away from us, sitting at a desk, listening to everything we said, even reacting a little, if I was reading my body language right.

Tree took a tentative step toward the boy.

"Son?" he said.

The boy was silent.

"Dr. Cash tells me you joined the exercise group this week. He says you're hanging right in there. I can't . . . can't tell you how happy that makes me."

The boy turned and smiled, almost imperceptibly, and turned back toward the window.

"Looks like you're putting on some weight. That starchy hospital food, I suppose. Good thing you're taking up that exercise thing."

The boy was silent.

"It'll be getting warm soon. Maybe we could get out and play some tennis together. Dr. Cash says there're some courts near here, and we could use one, if you like, when it warms up."

And it went on like that, for fifteen minutes, Tree struggling painfully to maintain the one-sided, small-talk conversation, while his son sat staring, reacting occasionally, usually with that small smile, but nothing more.

"Well," Tree said, finally, with reluctance, in relief, "gotta go now. See you next Monday. I . . . I love you, son."

The boy turned and nodded and turned away. Roger waved to us in the hall as we left. He was on his way back to Frank Jr.'s side.

I didn't ask Tree anything till we were out of there, iron doors shut behind us, in the cool outer corridor of the hospital.

"He never says anything?" I asked. "He just sits there and looks out the window and smiles now and then?"

Tree's eyes were glazed. "You don't know how much those smiles mean to me. It's taken him four months to get that far."

Half an hour later, in a bar in downtown Iowa City, Tree told me the story.

23

THE ONLY TIME business is slow in a college-town bar like the Airliner is when it's closed, but this was mid-afternoon and a quieter time than most, so it didn't make a bad place to talk. We bought drinks at the bar, a double Scotch straight up for Tree and a Coke on ice for me, and carried them to a booth at the rear.

Tree had a lot of lines in his face, which gave him a rough-hewn, Marlboro man quality capable of luring at least an occasional younger woman for a bounce on his water bed. At the moment, however, in the shadowy, flickering reflection of the candle in glass that lit the booth, those lines seemed simply a sign of age.

And his sigh said he felt even older than he looked.

"I didn't raise him," he said. "His mother did. I met her

in Reno, in '56 or 7. I was drifting back and forth between Vegas and Reno, working for casinos sometimes, sometimes for myself. I already knew what I wanted . . . my own place, why settle for less? I ran some joints for the DiPreta boys, in Des Moines, after the war. Learned everything there is about managing a club, any kind of a club. But there was no place to climb, there were enough DiPreta brothers to fill all the top slots in the Des Moines action, so I left. I liked to gamble and I was good at it. I started hitting poker games in little towns and big ones and everything between. Ended up on the Reno and Vegas circuit, of course. She was a cocktail waitress at Harold's. Nineteen and already divorced once, but no kids. I was dealing blackjack. Knocked her up, married her. I don't know why, except I always had it in the back of my head to have a kid, and she was a looker and I thought I loved her, the cunt. She had blond hair everywhere and tits that wouldn't stop and I'd fuck her today if I could and hate her while I was doing it."

He stopped for a moment, embarrassed. Scratched his head. Dandruff seemed his only grooming problem. He looked down at his drink. Drank it, got up and got another and drank half of that before going on.

"You know the first couple years weren't so bad. She loved Frank Jr. She was a good mother, no shit. And she was good to me. That was while I was out hustling my ass, making my goddamn fortune. Maybe that's why she put up such a good front, those first couple years. She must've known I had it in me to make it, and figured to stick with me till I did. We weren't married three years before I had my place on the river, across from Burlington, and it made money from day one, right away they were calling it Little Las Vegas, that little town we took over. I owned my own place and a piece of everybody else's on the street. The only help I had was the DiPretas. My old bosses backed me, at the start, but they stayed out of my way. You want another drink?"

"No."

He did.

This was hard for him and the lubrication was a must. Still, he seemed to feel the need to tell me all this, and not just because someone wanted him dead and to stop it I needed background. That was part of it, but important too was his need to tell *somebody*, to purge himself of memories too personal to tell anyone except a stranger.

He came back with a third double, drank it, and went on.

"She waited," he said, "waited till things were going real good for me, and then she filed the papers. She socked me for a ton of alimony, let me tell you, and child support, only that I didn't mind so much, the bitch. She took my kid and drained the fuck out of me, and my opinion of marriage ever since went down a little, you know? Never again. Anyway, she raised the kid, or her sister did. She was screwing a lot of guys, never did get married again, but then that'd stop the money, right? I'll never figure out why she was such a good mother at first and then just turned the kid over to that senile sister of hers. The only thing I can say for the twat is she let me see the kid, couple of weeks in the summer, Christmas, some other holiday, usually. I'd take him camping, ball game, things like that. I was a good father to him, good as I could be, considering what little chance I got. And he looked up to me. He really did. That made me feel good, and I'm not ashamed to say it. Another drink?"

"Not me," I said. "You have to drive back, remember."

"One more won't hurt."

Well, if it did, he sure didn't seem to feel it. He showed it only in the increased speed and ease of his speech, which wasn't slurred in the least.

"She turned into a sort of a lush, after a while," he said, his own glass empty now. "You get soft living on somebody else's money all the time, never working a day, you know? She never worked a day. Last fucking job she ever had was when she was a cocktail waitress at Harold's, in Reno, which is where I met her, the whore. That's what she turned into, only she *gave* it away. With all the money of mine she had, you'd think she'd at least go around fucking the country club set or something, but no. Lowlifes. That's what she was and who she liked to be around. Just pick up some goddamn factory worker in a bar and ball him and blow him and Jesus. Anyway, she got hit by a car about five, six, years ago. Drunk. And Frank Jr. came to live with me. He was torn, though, I think, you know? That sister-in-law of mine was the closest thing to a mother Frank ever had, and how can you blame him for feeling something for the old douche bag? Listen, I got to have a beer chaser, that's all there is to it. You?"

"Okay. Make it a gimlet, though."

He did, and he sipped some beer before starting up again.

"He was a quiet kid, Frank Jr. He wasn't too active, not in sports or any of those high school things. I think I maybe disappointed him, a little, because I was more strict than he thought I'd be. I wanted to know where he was going, what time he'd be in, things like that. I wanted to know what crowd he was running with, would check out the kids, their parents. He had some friends I didn't much approve of, but I finally gave up on that. He was his mother's son, after all, what're you gonna do? The biggest blow-up we ever had was over money. I didn't give him much. Hell, I didn't give him any. I put a roof over his head, food on his fucking table, and it was a goddamn good roof and the food wasn't leftovers by a long shot. I had a sixty-thousand-dollar home, there in Burlington, maid who cooked, kid had it easy. Too easy to suit me. I wanted him to work. He needed to know about that, that things don't come easy in this life. I didn't want him to be a lousy whore like his mother, if you know what I mean. You got to learn to earn your money, or at least fucking win it, you know what I mean? I tried to teach him that, and I think he came to learn it and maybe even respect me for it. He worked at a gas station and before you know it he had his own car and he dressed good and I was proud of the kid, really was. The only thing was I should've watched him closer. I just couldn't keep him from that crowd he ran with, and about two years ago it all kind of came to a head."

He paused. Sipped, then gulped at his beer. Draining it.

"I found this bag of grass in his room. Marijuana. Shit is what they call it, and I couldn't agree more. I showed it to him. He admitted he'd tried it. His friends insisted, he said. It was a pretty good-size bag and I enjoyed emptying the motherfucker down the toilet and flushing it in front of him. I didn't beat him or anything like that. I'm not that kind of father. But I had to do something."

He leaned forward.

"I looked into it a little and found out the high school Frank was going to was a pusher's paradise. . . . You could buy anything in that fucking place you wanted, anything you could buy in some fucking Chicago slum. I found out the junior high in town was the same, thirteen-year-old kids smoking grass and popping pills and I don't know what. There was nothing to do but get Frank the hell away from there. Why not, I figured. What better way. People had been wanting to buy me out since the second week I opened, and business had slacked off a little since the looser drinking law passed in Iowa, so it wasn't a bad business move getting out of there, either."

"So you came to Des Moines again," I said.

"Well, we moved to West Lake, that little town by the Barn, first. I bought a house. Frank Jr. enrolled at the new consolidated high school there, for his senior year. I got the Barn going and was making a profit before the dust settled."

"Sounds like a happy ending."

"I thought it was. Where I fucked up was I didn't spend more time with the boy. I was busy getting the Barn off the ground, and he was still a little sullen about me pulling him out of high school his last year, away from all his lowlife friends, so I was just sort of leaving him alone. Thought he'd work things out for himself."

"How did he do?"

He studied the flame in the glassed candle. "This time I didn't find it in his room. He stopped hiding things in his room, after the first time. This was in his car. Another bag of stuff."

"Grass again?"

"I wish it was. Grass isn't white, though, is it, Quarry? White fucking powder?"

"Christ," I said. "Your kid was shooting smack?"

"Evidently it hadn't got that far, thank God. The way I reconstruct it, he must've got in with some peckerheads from Des Moines who make his friends back home look like goddamn choir boys. I know for a fact he was using marijuana, right along, talked to some kids his age who went to school at West Lake with him, and they all knew what he was into, everybody knew but me. His peckerhead friends must've convinced him to turn onto the hard stuff about the time I stumbled in."

"What did you do about it?"

"Same as before, only this time I shoved his ass in the car and drove him to Iowa City and checked him into the Psychopathic Hospital and said, here, here's my kid, help him, he's got this drug problem. And later they told me he did . . . but not heroin. I found the goddamn stuff before he had a chance to use it, even once, and that's about the only break I got out of this fucking game. But he was psychologically addicted, they said, to marijuana."

"Is that why he doesn't say anything?"

"That's part of it. I guess. Even the peckerhead doctors don't know, really. You see, when I found that junk, I flushed it down the john, like the other time, and made him watch, too, like the other time, and while I was doing it, he said, 'Don't.' And that's the last thing I've heard him say. When he was first checked in, at the hospital, he talked to the doctors, other patients, but he was quiet, and gradually, over a period of a couple weeks, he pulled into a shell. Hasn't said a word."

"Frank," I said. Kindly. "I know this is something you're very concerned about, but how does it relate to you and me?"

"I think it does relate." He looked convinced, like Oral Roberts telling his audience God is not dead. "I've stepped on people, Quarry. I've made some enemies. But that's, most of it, past history. This is a recent history."

And he took a clipping out of his pocket. The date was recent, about a month old; the headline: CITIZEN GROUP LAUNCHES ATTACK ON DRUGS, with a smaller headline above saying: Young People Major Victim. The article told of a civic group whose initials were D.O.P.E. (Des Moines Organization of Parental Enquiry) and who were demanding action on the "rampant drug problem demoralizing the youth of our city, state and country," in the words of the ex-mayor who headed the "Executive Council" of the group.

I gave the clipping back to him. I looked at him close, in hopes he was kidding. He wasn't.

"I'm staying on the sidelines, naturally . . . but it was my idea, my money, my connections got this thing going. I got some very influential friends, rich people, well-to-do assholes who don't like the idea of their kids being stuck in the same school with a bunch of nigger junkies, and who're willing to put their money where their mouth is and help cause a stink and put a stop to it. It's a matter of educating the public, finger-fucking the press, all that Ralph Nader lobby group bullshit. Of course the group can only do so much, but I can put pressure on by myself, with the people I know in politics, local and state and even federal, and people in law enforcement, all kinds of people I got influence with."

"You're kind of an unlikely candidate for civic reformer, aren't you, Frank?"

"Look, I know dope's just a business, like anything else. Of course I never fucked with it myself, or any people I worked with, either, the DiPretas, say, they never had their hands in that kind of shit. A lot of mob people never did get into it, and hardly no mob people are into it, anymore. It's the niggers and spicks who own it, now, but even so, I know I'm not gonna single-handed wipe out dope in the world, and couldn't care less if I did. I just want to cause some trouble for the fucking leeches who turned a decent kid into a vegetable, all right? And I must be pulling it off, and it looks like, even though I kept in the background on this thing, word's out I'm the one who put the heat on." He shrugged. "So somebody bought a contract."

"That's what somebody did," I said.

"Anyway, they're two different things entirely."

"What?"

"Running a gambling house and selling poison."

"Right," I said.

And finished my drink.

24

SHE WAS HALF asleep and completely naked, sheets and covers twisted and not covering much of her at all. She was on her stomach but turned to one side, hugging a pillow, against which rested one generous breast, cuddled there, not squashed, its large dark nipple soft and smooth and delicate, a flower with its petals unfolded. Her face, sans make-up, looked young, almost child-like, except for the worldly cast of those eyes and the faint smile of the freshly fucked. She lay there, dark blond hair tickling her shoulders, beads of sweat glistening along the sweep of her slender back, legs sprawled but gracefully so, slopes of her ass spread gently, exposing wisps of pubic hair and a glimpse or two of pink and one firm creamy thigh.

Often, in the clinical light of post-coital moments, a man

may notice for the first time a pimple on a formerly perfect ass, or a dark coarse hair growing along the edge of a nipple, or how her one breast seems now oddly smaller than the other one, or the redness from the elastic around panty hose, or a scar or stretch marks or a birthmark, and pretty soon he can't remember what was the big deal.

Lu was what every man is looking for: a woman who looked as good after as before.

I brought her a cup of Sanka. I brought myself one, too.

She looked up at me with hooded eyes, still hugging her pillow. "People are supposed to smoke afterwards, don't you know that? Not drink instant coffee."

"I say if you can't smoke during, why bother?"

She laughed. Her laugh was throaty, baritone, like her voice. "You know," she said, leaning on an elbow, "I used to smoke. I gave it up. Had an uncle who died from it."

"Cigarettes killed my mother."

"No kidding? That's terrible."

"Yeah. She got hit by a Chesterfields truck."

"Go to hell," she said, showing her gums as she smiled. "Gimme that goddamn coffee."

She sat up in bed, took the coffee, draping a sheet over her lap, for decorum's sake, I guess. I wondered how decorum would feel about those two big naked boobs.

"Seriously, though, folks," I said, sitting by her on the bed, "I like it that you don't smoke. It's nice to taste a girl's mouth that tastes like a girl's mouth. Kissing some women is like sucking a tailpipe."

"It's the same with men. Fucks your teeth up, too."

"It's too bad everybody can't be clean-cut like us."

"Fuckin' shame. Hey, you haven't said how your job interview went, this afternoon."

That was the story I told her. I even told her I was going

to the Amanas, to see about a job selling the refrigerators and shit they make there. It was now about six, and I'd been back half an hour.

"I won't know for a while," I said.

"Don't you even have a gut reaction to the interview or the job?"

"Sure I got a gut reaction. I think it sounds like a crazy job, and the guy I talked to was also crazy, but I'll probably take it anyway."

"Is that desperation talking, or just apathy?"

"Protestant work ethic, I think. How'd you spend your day off?"

"Like I thought I would: shopping. Didn't you see the packages and sacks and stuff on the kitchen table?"

Like I was supposed to?

"Well, since you're probably broke, why don't I take you out to dinner? I understand Riccelli's has terrific pasta."

"They do," she said, "only . . ."

"Only?"

"We already have plans."

"We?"

"You and me. You remember us, don't you, Jack?"

"Vaguely. But I seem to have forgotten our plans."

"That's because I haven't told them to you yet. Anyway, you're finally going to get to meet Ruthy."

We hadn't had time to see Ruthy after the Sunday performance at the Candle Lite, because Lu had to get to the Barn to work. It was about time I met her bosom buddy . . . and Tree's. I still hadn't broken the news to Tree, yet, about his current bed partner being a pal of the woman who was the surveilling half of a hit team that probably included a certain guy who was lousy at cards and good at smashing lamps in people's faces.

"Where are we going to meet her?" I asked.

"Another Italian restaurant that's supposed to be good. Downtown. It's called DiPreta's. Heard of it?"

"Yeah. Family restaurant, isn't it?"

She didn't catch my joke, or pretended not to. Instead she just nodded and said, "We'll be meeting her there around midnight."

"Midnight? Midnight as in six hours from now?"

"That's right. We can have some popcorn at the show, if you're so hungry."

"What show is that?"

"The one you're taking me to, as soon as we get dressed."

"What show are we going to?"

"I thought I'd let you pick it."

"I don't know if I can handle all this responsibility."

"Go fuck yourself."

"That would be an even bigger responsibility."

"The paper's on the kitchen counter. See what movies are playing and what the times are."

I did.

I suggested a Clint Eastwood double feature, which she rejected as too violent. I pointed out that we had a lot of time to kill, and we settled on a Woody Allen double feature.

I watched her get dressed.

"Do you own any kind of underwear except transparent?" I asked her.

"Nobody else has complained."

"It's just that I got a sample case someplace of real lacy things that you could have, if you wanted them. You know. If you ever were feeling feminine or something."

"Is this feminine enough for you?" she asked, grinning, giving me the finger.

"I'll just take you up on that," I said, and a while later we were having some more instant coffee, and I said, "Why midnight?"

"It's the first chance Ruthy'll have to get away. It's strike weekend."

"Strike weekend?"

"Sunday was the last day for *Born Yesterday*. A new play opens Wednesday, *The Fourposter*, I think."

"That's some explanation."

"Don't you know what strike means?"

"Sure. Strike a match, strike it rich, the Teamsters . . ."

"It means, like, strike the sets. They tear down all the old sets and put up new ones, one play making room for the next."

"Why's an actress like your friend Ruthy involved in that?"

"It's a repertory company. Everybody works both back stage and on. You can be lead in one play and prop man in the next. On strike weekend they work their butts off."

"Interesting. Well. I guess we better try to get dressed again."

"Right. Hey, I almost forgot."

"What?"

"We just might be able to line up that job at the Barn for you, tonight."

"Why's that?"

"Ruthy's boyfriend's going to be there, too. This'll come as a shock to you, but her boyfriend happens to be Frank Tree himself."

"You got to be kidding," I said.

25

I PARKED AROUND the corner from DiPreta's Italian Restaurant, which was on a one-way that I couldn't turn onto coming from the direction of Lu's apartment, and as we were getting out of the car, the blue Chevelle I'd noticed following us on the way over slid by innocently and pulled into a place half a block up. The guy was either new at this or a moron. Both, maybe.

"You go on ahead," I said to her.

"Why?"

"Tell you later. Please go ahead."

She made a shrugging face and got out of the car and walked. When she'd disappeared around the corner, I leaned over and got the nine-millimeter out of the glove compartment, checked it over to see if it had been fucked with, stuck it in my belt. I was wearing a sportshirt and slacks but the night was cool enough to require a light jacket and the jacket covered the gun.

This took a couple of minutes and in that time the sidewalk on my side of the street stayed clear. It stayed clear on the other side, too. Midnight Monday in Des Moines isn't exactly rush hour.

The little moron in the Chevelle was sitting tight, waiting for me to do something.

I did something.

I got out of the GT and walked, slowly, and before I turned the corner I heard a car door open and shut somewhere not far behind me.

Christ, what a loser.

DiPreta's was down at the far end of the block, half of which it encompassed, an alley separating the restaurant from the other half block of commercial buildings. I turned down the alley, making no secret of it, but then picked up speed and about a third-way down stepped into a recessed doorway that had just enough room for me and three garbage cans. I took the lid off one of the cans and when the guy walked by hit him in the face with it.

He staggered back a step, seemed to momentarily regain his composure, then did a belly flop on the brick alley floor. He hit like a wet sack of sand.

I turned him over.

He looked familiar. Naggingly so.

He was average size, average build, wearing a dark ribbed sweater over a light pressed shirt, brushed denim slacks, almost collegiate-looking. He had short blond hair, ordinary features, his large ears being the only distinguishing feature he had. That and the broken nose the garbage can lid had given him.

I'd seen him before, no question, but where?

Wherever, he wasn't anybody I'd paid any attention to. I'd been half expecting that sullen young prick from the Barn, the house dealer who I was so sure had smashed that lamp in my face. In fact that was why I'd put so much oomph behind the garbage can lid. I wondered if I'd decked some poor schmuck who just happened to be on his way to the same restaurant, at the same time, as Lu and me.

Then it came to me.

He was from the Barn. Not the guy I'd expected, but someone else I'd seen there; not a house dealer, but a regular. A clown who'd been there every night, and who liked to play five-card stud but didn't have the balls for too high stakes, though he didn't play badly, if I recalled right.

I checked his billfold. There was a couple hundred bucks in there, and it might have been mine, so I pocketed it. He had a driver's license, too. It said he was from Santa Barbara, California, and that he was twenty-eight. And here's the good part: his name was John Smith.

Well, I guess somebody has to be named John Smith. And I figured that's who this guy was, because nobody, not even a little moron, picks a phony name that obvious.

He also had no gun. No weapon of any kind. Not even a goddamn pen knife.

Something was starting to tingle on the back of my neck. It was a bad feeling and it was spreading. Something was very, very wrong here.

My still unconscious friend was clearly not a professional anything. His idea of shadowing you was to tailgate; he was unarmed; and his name was either the worst alias in the world or maybe just proof he was some poor, dumb, bland-looking son of a bitch named John Smith from Santa Barbara, California.

Shit. The numbers here were not adding up. If the former Glenna Cole, current Lucille was the stakeout, and that prick dealer from the Barn was the hitter, where the hell did John Smith fit in?

The frustrating thing was I couldn't just shake him awake and have a talk with him and find out. Talking to him meant I might have to kill him when I was done, and I didn't want to do any killing right now. Killing him would perhaps tell certain people something about me I didn't want them to know; leaving him alive, as the possible victim of a mugging, might make it necessary for the jury on me to stay out a while longer.

So I had to be content with stuffing him ass first in a garbage can and leaving him to wake up and wonder, after which I returned to my car, left the nine-millimeter in the glove compartment, and walked back to the restaurant to meet Frank Tree for the first time.

26

THE OUTSIDE OF the place was classy-looking charcoal-colored brick with white mortar. There was more brick inside, but whorehouse-red brocade wallpaper dominated. And that's the whole story of DiPreta's Italian Restaurant: it was alternately sleazy and luxurious, as plush as the backseat of a millionaire's limo, as tasteless as a girl whose panties have the day of the week on them.

Lu was waiting for me just beyond the huge .wooden front doors, with their elaborate carved wood handles shaped like rearing, roaring lions (you grabbed a lion around the belly to pull open a door), and she looked genuinely worried.

"What was that all about?" she wanted to know.

"I thought somebody was following us," I said.

We walked past the area in front where some guys in white outfits and chef hats were making pizzas in front of the street window, the pizza ovens built of that same fancy charcoal-color brick, and moved into the subdued lighting of the dining area.

"*Was* somebody following us?"

"Yes," I said.

A lady in her forties wearing a dark red evening gown and a white corsage, with dark black brittle hair piled as high as a small child, and a mole as black as her hair next to a mouth as red as her dress in a face as white as her corsage, said, "Party of two?" and Lu told her we were with the Tree party and the lady asked us to walk this way, and I resisted the urge to turn that into an even bigger joke than it already was.

There were booths on either side of us, as we walked, and each booth had its own tiffany shade hanging lamp and its own original oil painting, which ran to matadors and still lifes and crying clowns and big-eyed children and frozen summer landscapes. We followed the lady in red into a large open area, where a mammoth cut-glass chandelier was suspended which no one seemed anxious to stand under, with an ornate bar off to the left, the prerequisite reclining-nude oil painting in the midst of an obscenely well-stocked series of wine and liquor racks, and an open stairway rising before us to reveal the second floor, or anyway a hallway thereof, with more oil paintings and the closed doorways to banquet rooms, apparently, and we went off to the right, to a private nook (or was it a cranny?) where Frank Tree and Ruthy sat at a table big enough for twelve.

"Jack Wilson, Frank Tree," Lu said.

Tree stood and extended a hand and I shook it. If he was surprised, he didn't show it.

He said, "I've seen you around, Jack. You been winning some money off me, if I'm not mistaken."

I said he wasn't and sat down.

Ruthy raised a hand to boob level and milled her fingers in a sort of wave. "I'm Ruthy," she said.

"I guessed," I said.

She gave me a schoolgirl grin and said, "I've heard a lot about you, Jack."

"If it isn't bad, it isn't true," I said.

We were in the middle of the big table. I was across from Ruthy, who was wearing a yellow short-sleeve sweatshirt that had a dancing Snoopy on it. Her blond hair was pulled back from her face and she had little make-up on. She looked good, though. Nice tits. Lu looked good, too, in her pants suit with the halter top. Tree was wearing a sportcoat and open-collar shirt, and seemed to have sobered up considerably since this afternoon. The range of clothing at the table was in keeping with the rest of the patrons at DiPreta's; there was everything from evening wear to sandals and sweatshirts and all the stops between. It was like being on Mars, or in Cleveland.

A middle-aged waitress in traditional black-and-white uniform with black hose came over to take our order, asking first if we wanted anything from the bar. Tree and I both declined, but Lu asked for a Bloody Mary and Ruthy a screwdriver. Then Tree recommended the rigatoni and Lu and I went along with him, but Ruthy wanted an anchovy pizza.

When the waitress had gone, I told Ruthy how much I enjoyed the play Sunday.

"Did you really?" It lit up her dark blue eyes, which darted around as she spoke, never looking at you, never landing. "It's too bad you couldn't see me in something heavy. I mean, *Born Yesterday*, after all. How shallow can you get? Anyway at least it was fun, and, well, you can't go dropping Edward Albee in the laps of these little old ladies in tennis shoes at the matinees, can you?"

"I wouldn't," I said.

"Not that anybody in Des Moines is ready for something heavy." She shook a Virginia Slims out of the pack in front of her; she'd already had several. Tree used a lighter to fire it for her. "The theater's a once-or-twice-a-year thing for Des Moines—birthday, anniversary. . . . Before curtain the manager comes out and has everybody in the house applaud for people celebrating 'special days.' But you know that. You were there. Bunch of smalltown bullshit, but what can you expect? Now this *Fourposter* play coming up isn't so bad, but I'm not in it. A good woman's role for a change, too. I guess I'll be playing these lousy ingénues and sexpot roles till my teeth fall the fuck out. It'd be nice to play something sensitive for a change. Like when I was at Drake."

"Drake?"

"The university here. I did a lot of good stuff there. I did *Rhinoceros.*"

"I don't think I know it."

"It's a wonderful play. It's about everybody turning into rhinoceroses."

"Sounds nice."

"Oh, it is. It's very symbolic."

"What of?"

She gestured with her cigarette. "Uh, people getting insensitive, I think. People turning into monsters and nobody noticing or caring and pretty soon everybody's a monster. Our director at the time said it was about Vietnam, even though it was written before Vietnam. I think it's about conformity. It's a comedy."

"I like a good laugh."

"I played an ingénue in that, too, but at least the play was heavy. There are so few good roles for women. That's because most of the playwrights are men. If it wasn't for the queer ones, we wouldn't have any decent roles."

I started to ask something and Lu, who knew I was leading Ruthy on, cut in.

"How's your work coming?" she said. "Those sets struck yet, kiddo?"

"God, no, and we been working all day without a real break and am I famished. And here we sit in the slowest restaurant in town, and it'll be years before the food comes. We really should've gone to Babe's or Noah's."

"Then why'd we come here?" I asked.

"First, some friends of Frank's own the place and even at the busy times we get a private place to eat, and second, they got the best anchovy pizza in town."

Tree had been silent through all of this. He'd been watching Ruthy throughout, hanging on her every word, savoring everything about her with that special fatherly sort of lust that gives incest a bad name.

And she was a fine-looking girt. She had a lot going for her besides her chest, too. There was a fascinating mouth on the child, a fascination having nothing at all to do with the words that came out of said mouth. Puffy, pouty lips and little white teeth. It was easy to imagine that mouth doing things other than eating an anchovy pizza.

But watching her eat the pizza, once it came, wasn't especially fascinating. She wolfed it down and kept up her chatter as she did, which was impressive in its way, but a sexy girl eating with her mouth open is just as obnoxious as if it were you or me.

Between bites of rigatoni I asked her how she and Lucille met.

"We got together down in Florida," Ruthy said. "We lived in the same apartment building. I was working a dinner theater down there. I was there a year. You should've seen my tan. But I got a chance a couple years ago to move back to Des Moines and work the Candle Lite, and Des Moines is sort of home to me, since I went to college here, before I dropped out, so I was glad to come back . . . even if it meant kissing my year-round tan goodbye."

Tree finally decided to join the conversation. "The nice thing about the Candle Lite, for Ruthy," he said, "is she gets to work other places, too. The Candle Lite is linked with a number of other dinner theaters in the Midwest, and in many of them she gets to appear with name actors. Just last March she was in Milwaukee in *The Seven Year Itch* with one of the actors from *Gilligan's Island*."

"It usually keeps me out of the *hard* work," Ruthy said, feigning sheepishness. "This is actually the first time I've had to help strike a set since I came to the Candle Lite . . . which is why I'm working so hard at it. The rest of the company thinks I'm going to loaf my way through it, and I'm going to show 'em."

"Not to change the subject," Lu said, apparently a bit bored with Ruthy's show biz patter, "but Jack here's been looking for work for the past week or so and hasn't had much luck. Jack has better manners than to bring it up now, but I'm not a shy type. Think you might have something for him at the Barn?"

"What line are you in, Jack?" Tree said. Nothing in his voice, but a little something in his eyes.

"I'm a salesman. I used to sell ladies underwear, but you can see how much the girls here care about that."

The air was chill in there and four nice nipples were standing out and we all laughed a little.

"Well, I know what kind of poker player you are. And I'm thinking of replacing one of my dealers. Interested?"

"Very."

"Come around and play some cards tomorrow night . . . and try not to win too much more of my money . . . and stay and talk to me after closing."

"Fine."

Just as we'd prearranged.

Then I asked Ruthy how exactly "striking a set" was accomplished, and she told us. Tree and I listened intently. Lu had a couple of Bloody Marys and stared off someplace.

27

ON THE STAGE was an antique oak bed, a post rising from
each corner to support a lace-trimmed, blue satin canopy.
There were several other pieces of antique-looking
furniture, a chair, table, trunk; another chair, and all of
them, including the bed, were pushed forward, almost to
the edge of the stage, as Ruthy and another member of the
repertory company, a lumpish female in curlers and
workshirt and rolled-up jeans, painted the light blue
"walls" of the set, which had a doorway off to the left and a
window to the right.

It was mid-morning and the front doors of the Candle
Lite Playhouse had been open. I walked up the short flight
of stairs onto the stage, where day before yesterday I had
filled a plate with food, and my footsteps clumped hollowly
on the floor of the stage.

Ruthy, on her hands and knees painting, turned and looked up at me and said, "Hi! Where's Lucille?"

"The apartment," I said. "She kicked me out. She had a bunch of cleaning to do."

(Which made it convenient for both of us, as I could go do the snooping I needed to, and Lu could continue her surveillance of Tree, without either of us getting in the other's way. And since I knew Frank Tree would not be leaving his apartment before nightfall and the Barn, and would in fact be spending the day in front of his television with a revolver in his lap—with time out only for bodily functions and perhaps the preparation and consumption of a TV dinner—I had few worries about what might happen while I was out.)

Ruthy was, like her lumpy companion, wearing jeans and a workshirt. Ruthy's jeans, however, were tourniquet tight, and her workshirt knotted into a halter, leaving a succulent tummy, complete with navel, exposed, the buttons at the top open and giving me a skyscraper look down her impressive cleavage. It was a view she was aware of, and even exploited. Whether she was just a cock-tease in general, or had something in mind for me specifically, was, like my teased cock, up in the air.

She gave me a sly look that I had seen before (in her performance Sunday) and said, "Sure she isn't cheating on you? It wouldn't take twenty minutes to clean that place of hers stem to stern."

I squatted down to talk with her and look her in the eye and not the gland.

"Lu's like anybody else," I said. "She's just got to have a little privacy sometimes, and she's got a right to it. It's her apartment. I'm just a guest."

"Well, if I had a guest at home like you, I wouldn't send you out in the cold."

"It's not so cold. In fact the sun's out for a change. Kind of a nice day out there. Too bad you're stuck in here working."

"Oh I don't mind. It's all a part of theater. It's just as exciting to me to be backstage as center-stage."

The lumpish girl, standing, stroking with a paint brush, rolled her eyes, without Ruthy seeing.

"Did you tell Lucille you were gonna stop by and see me?"

"No," I said.

"I'm gonna be busy all day, Jack."

"I figured you might be. I'll tell you why I stopped by. I noticed in your program, Sunday, that there's something called Candle Lite Productions, that does advertising work, locally. TV and radio spots, that sort of thing."

"That's right. This place used to be a church that did its own radio shows here. There's a studio set-up on the second floor, where we do the recording. Why?"

"I thought maybe I could pick up some extra work. I thought your production company might be able to use a salesman, part-time, maybe?"

"Well, Jack, it's not my production company, but I sure can talk to the boss lady for you. She's here, now, if you want to see if you can see her."

"That'd be great."

"I'll go get her for you. Give me about fifteen minutes. She's probably just finishing her breakfast about now, and might not be dressed yet."

"She lives here?"

"Sure. So do I. There's four apartments here. She uses one, her ex-husband who manages the place has another, and me and another permanent member of the troupe use the other two. When I say I *live* in the theater, I ain't kidding, booby. Be back in a flash. A fifteen-minute flash, that is."

She stood up. Her jeans were so tight they were sucked up into her pubis. It was a wonder she could walk in the damn things, but she did, and then I was alone with her stocky coworker, who put down her paint brush and said, "Buy you a cup of coffee, friend?"

I took her up on it, and soon we were sitting at a ringside table, drinking instant coffee. Her name was Martha and she had pretty features buried in a pale round face and smoked two Camels in rapid succession as we talked.

"You want some free advice?" she asked.

"Price is right," I shrugged.

"Stay away from that little cunt."

I acted surprised by her language, then pretended to recover and said, "Well, I doubt it's little. I get the idea she gives it plenty of exercise."

"That she does. But you get my drift. I'm talking figurative cunts, not literal. And that's a figurative cunt if I ever met one."

"I've met a few myself. What makes her qualify?"

"You know that innocent, dumb, sexy blonde act of hers? Well, it is just an act. She comes on that way to the guys in the company, except for those she's had in the sack a few times who she gives the cold shoulder once she's bored and who come to hate her guts as much as the women, some of whom she comes on to too, though to most she's shit personified from the start. The pits, my friend."

"How so?"

"Aloof. Conceited ass, first class. The cunt thinks she's Glenda Jackson and she isn't even Mamie Van Doren. The pissy part is she gets all the good roles, or most of 'em, anyway. She really must've fucked her way into somebody important's heart."

"Isn't she striking the set, like anybody else in the company?"

"That's just what I mean. This is the first time since she came here she ever lowered herself to that. I don't know how she rates, playing all those other dinner theaters all over, I mean that just isn't done. You're either part of a rep company or you aren't. You got to be a name to be on the circuit. Unless you fucked somebody important, I guess. Look, I probably shouldn't be telling you all this, but I heard you guys talking, I mean I was standing right there . . . and if you're shacked up with somebody already, don't throw it away for her. Look the other way when she comes on to you. Ignore the cunt. She just isn't worth it. Whatever you got now, it's better. Believe me."

"Thanks."

"Don't mention it. Besides," she said, pulling some smoke up in her head and letting it out her nose, "she isn't even all that hot in bed."

I thought about that a while, and went back to the bar where the hot water was and made myself a fresh cup of coffee. Martha came along. She was starting on her third Camel.

"I hate these things," she said, referring to the cigarette. "If I had a left nut, I'd give it for one goddamn half-smoked roach."

"I hear it's hard to score in this towm."

Which I really *had* heard, having spent an hour on the East Side trying to score myself, before coming here this morning. The closest I came was a black guy in a khaki outfit in front of a place called Soulful Record Shop who said maybe next week. Things were as lean as Tree had said. The local anti-drugs campaign seemed pretty effective, from my superficial investigation, at least.

"Hard to score?" she said. "No harder than shaking oleo out of a dairy farmer. Haven't you seen those hokey posters in the storefront windows? And heard the bullshit on the tube? And on the radio, and in the papers . . . D.O.P.E.? If ever an organization was aptly named, that's it. You wanna know the ironic part?"

"What's that?"

"Des Moines is supposed to be a sort of retirement village for Mafia types. Yeah. You can't turn around in Des Moines without bumping into an Italian restaurant, did you notice? Even the food served here at the Candle Lite is catered by one of them."

"I don't see your point."

"It's just kind of funny. These Mafia types move out of Chicago and places like that and come to nice, quiet Des Moines to retire, to watch their grandkids grow up in zero crime rate. Only they can't escape what they put in motion, you know? I wonder how many of these butts shouting law and order, how many of these D.O.P.E.s are Mafia types who started the problem themselves?"

It was a mice irony, but when I questioned her about it further, gently, she said it was just rumors. She wasn't a Des Moines native, and only knew what she'd heard longer-time residents say.

"Hey, Jack!" Ruthy said, moving toward us remarkably quickly, considering the tight jeans. "The boss lady says she'll see you, now."

And Ruthy put an arm around my waist and showed me the way.

28

A STAIRWAY OFF the lobby took us to the second floor, where the living, quarters and offices were. That is, all of them except Ruthy's; her small apartment was downstairs, in the basement of the place.

The door she led me to said PRIVATE on it. She knocked, a tenor voice within said, "Yeah," and we went in, Ruthy first.

It was a small office, just big enough for a metal desk with wood top, a few files, a few chairs and several walls of plaques and framed citations and some signed photographs of moderately well-known actors. The only wall that wasn't that way, besides the one with a door on it, was the bookcase wall, and the shelves of that were top-heavy with trophies. There were a few books, too, paperbacks mostly, and hardcovers on the careers of movie stars.

The woman was drinking orange juice, sitting behind the desk, which had nothing on it except a little brown box with a face the time appeared on, rolling along like the odometer of a car.

She was about thirty-five and looked about forty-five, a cadaverously thin woman with an intelligent, unattractive face; her dark brown, almost black eyes were penetrating, demanding of attention, although she kept them constantly stiffed, eyes so commanding they diverted from her sunken, pockmarked cheeks, hook nose and well-kept but painfully thin colorless brown hair, which she wisely wore short.

She was wearing a bathrobe, light blue and softly quilted and rather feminine, but not in the blatant way Ruthy's tight jeans and plunging neckline were.

"I'm Christine Price, Mr. Wilson."

She extended her arm across the desk like a spear. I took the hand she offered, shook it, gave it back. She had a firm grip. She was skinny but I wouldn't want to arm wrestle her.

"Please call me Jack," I said and took a chair.

"Jack, then. I prefer Christine, to Chris, and Ms. Wilson to Mrs. But you call me what you like."

"Christine, then."

"Good," she smiled. A toothy white smile that was so honest and engaging I almost didn't notice it was grotesque.

"I understand you do advertising work, here," I said, and we were off and running.

Ruthy sat and listened quietly, palms pressed together and slipped down between her thighs against her box, a posture of innocence that evoked the opposite.

I told Christine Price that I imagined their clients had been largely in the Des Moines area itself, advertisers drawn to the Candle Lite production company, because it was an arm of the first professional theater group in Des Moines, whose good reputation and high visibility in the community were all the selling necessary, locally. She told me I was right. I told her how a man on the road could extend their market to the entire state, and probably to surrounding states as well. She wanted to know how. Various ways, I said. By playing tapes of radio commercials produced by Candle Lite to potential clients, and showing films or video tapes of television commercials; by accumulating letters of references from satisfied Des Moines clients, and having photographs to show taken during production of both radio and TV commercials, and perhaps some taken at the theater at a performance, showing off particularly impressive sets and a packed house, neither of which directly related to advertising work but both of which spoke of professionalism and were just generally impressive, especially in the hands of a good salesman. Which I claimed to be. It was a pretty good spiel. Christine Price seemed to think so, too. Anyway she leaned forward across her desk, listening.

She also smoked a skinny cigar that didn't smell too terrific, but made her feel like an executive, I guess, so what the hell.

I was glad she seemed to believe me, because if she did, chances were Ruthy did, too. And all of this was more for Ruthy's benefit than anybody else's, as she would surely report this conversation to Lu, hopefully confirming me as a real person actually out looking for work, maybe making me a little less suspicious.

It also gave me an excuse to be here, at the Candle Lite, my real reason being to check up on Ruthy; but to do that properly I needed to get rid of her and talk to the boss lady in private. And I could see no way of doing that.

But then Christine Price did me a favor.

"Ruthy," she said, "I believe your friend Jack, here, and I are going to talk some hard business. And I think we'd best be left alone for that, if you don't mind."

"I got some sets to paint," Ruthy said cheerfully, leaning over and patting me on the upper thigh, and got up and left.

And her boss came around the desk and sat on top of it, crossing her legs, showing a knee and a couple of calves. She didn't have bad legs for an ugly woman.

"What kind of experience have you had?" she asked.

"I had a nice childhood."

She smiled coquettishly. "I mean as a salesman."

"I was a salesman for five years. A little longer than that actually. Before that I was in Vietnam."

"You must be about thirty."

"About."

"What did you sell? How many firms did you work for?"

"Just one firm. Ladies underwear."

She liked that.

She said, "You look like somebody who wouldn't have much trouble getting in a woman's pants."

So that was her game. She wanted to be a man, wanted to play the employer role, but she wanted it all the way: she wanted to sleep with her secretary like any good boss.

"Actually I don't look that hot in women's pants," I said. "I don't have the build for it."

She gave me that toothy smile again and said, "Can I offer some friendly advice? It's free."

This was starting to sound familiar. "Price is right," I shrugged.

"Ruthy."

"What about her?"

"Be a little careful of her."

"Just a little?"

"Maybe a lot. She says you met Frank Tree last night. That you play cards and may do some dealing for him."

"That's right. I prefer a selling job, though. That's why I'm here."

"Ruthy's been thick with him, lately. How much do you know about him?"

"Frank Tree? Nothing."

"He's got some connections."

"Is that why I should be careful of Ruthy?"

"No. Not really. She's got some connections herself."

Something happened in her face, then; something turned it blank.

But only for a moment, after which she uncrossed her legs and lowered them to the floor and leaned her butt against the desk and folded her arms. The intense, businesslike look was back on her face.

"I like your idea," she said. "I think I could use you."

I'll bet.

"I'm glad to hear that," I said.

"Let me sleep on it Get back to me tomorrow, or sometime later this week and we'll talk it all out. Here. Here's my card, with my personal number."

She gave me a business card and I put it away.

"I'm sure we'll work something out," she said.

"Fine."

There was an awkward silence and I realized, suddenly, I'd been dismissed.

"Well," I said. "Thanks for the advice."

She went behind the desk and smiled flatly and looked down at its smooth empty surface, as if there were invisible papers that needed straightening.

I left, wondering what exactly had unnerved her. Made

her cut short both business interview and seduction attempt. I hadn't said enough myself to cause that. It had to be something she said. Something she let slip . . .

In the lobby, on my way out, I saw Martha on the way to the ladies' john.

I blew her a kiss.

"What was that for?" she said, with a silly grin.

"That' s for being the only female in this goddamn place that doesn't think of me as a mere sex object."

She said get outa here and I did.

29

I WAS SITTING in the same booth as that first night, in the Roy Rogers room upstairs at the Red Barn Club. It was just after six, and I'd again ordered the ribs and wondered idly if they'd be better than mediocre this time.

Lu had to be at work by six, and I hadn't got back to the apartment till five, so there'd been no time to eat at home. She didn't mind, as she claimed to be on a diet anyway (though there was no fat on her that I could see, at least none that I wanted her to be rid of), and she was downstairs working, presently, while I was upstairs eating.

I'd spent the afternoon further checking out the dope scene in Des Moines. I'd wandered the East Side some more, had risked my ass in a black pool hall in a section that came as close to being a ghetto as anything in the city and bordered the Drake campus area, where I tried some of the college hangouts. Finally I went to West Des Moines, a suburb whose downtown was dominated by antique shops and other oddball places of business, where hippie types were highly visible but not high. It was the same everywhere. Nothing to be had. Not a pill to pop, not a token toke. Oh, there was undoubtedly a small supply, accessible only to ingrained members of the local underground community. But the D.O.P.E. crackdown was real. Frank Tree really was something of a social reformer. It was enough to rekindle my beliefs in the basic goodness of America. Or make me want to throw up. One of the two.

When I was finished with the salad, a gimlet arrived, a practical joke sent up by my lady bartender, who had made it extra strong knowing I liked my gimlets just the opposite. I drank it anyway, and the ribs came and I started in on them and they were just as mediocre as the other time.

Mediocre or not, I ate all the food they put in front of me (Tree was picking up the tab, after all) and, as she cleared the table, had a peek down my characteristically busty Barn waitress's blouse for dessert. Then I tried to open the shutters on the window next to me, before remembering too late they were permanently closed. I stood and parted the ruffled curtains above the shutters and looked out at the parking lot. It was too early for there to be many cars. One of the perhaps twenty that were out there was a familiar-looking Chevelle.

I sat back down and thought about that, wondering if the Chevelle's driver was downstairs right now, a guy with a nose recently remodeled by a garbage can lid.

I went down to find out.

Only a few of the green baise-covered cardtables were in use this early in the evening. A blackjack table, and the five-card stud table. Most of the action was at the bar, people getting a little oiled before getting down to it.

The guy I was looking for wasn't in the room. But a probable friend of his was.

The sullen little cocksucker in glasses was sitting alone at the table where he nightly dealt draw, shuffling his cards.

I went over and sat down next to him.

"How's it going?" I said.

His eyes flicked up at me, then returned to watching his hands work the cards.

"It's going," he said.

What a sweetheart.

"Mind if I take a little money from you tonight?" I asked.

"You can try."

"Why should it be any harder tonight than any other night?"

He shrugged.

"You can go blind from that," I said.

"From what."

"From playing with yourself."

He said nothing. Just shuffled.

"Practice up good, now," I said, and left him.

I'd been trying to bait him, but he wasn't biting. In the past I'd made a point of being at least noncommittal to him, sometimes treating him damn near friendly. This should have jolted him a little. That permanent foul mood of his usually flared when people got smart with him, and he normally would've fired a cutting remark back. Why had he remained so passive? Still not the friendliest fucker in the world, but he'd barely reacted. Was it because it was me? Or was it something else?

I went over to the bar and Lu said, "How'd you like your drink?"

"Terrific. It tasted like an alcohol rub."

"We aim to please."

"Is Tree in his office?"

"Yes, but weren't you going to wait till after closing to talk to him?"

"I changed my mind."

"Go ahead, then. It's that door over to the right. Just knock."

I did, and Tree's voice behind the heavy wood door asked who it was and I told him.

He buzzed me in.

I shut the door behind me and sat in the chair in front of his desk, which had a portable color TV on it, some copies of *Playboy*, *Penthouse*, and *Hustler*, and a tall glass of what was apparently Scotch and maybe some water.

It was a plain, even drab office, with barnwood paneling, a room the size a doctor examines you in and with the same sort of warmth. Besides the big metal desk and the chairs we were sitting in, the room was bare. Except for a big old iron safe that squatted in the corner to the right of Tree like the fat lady at the circus.

Tree turned down the sound on the *Untouchables* rerun he was watching.

"Change of plans, Quarry?" he asked. "I thought we were going to talk later."

"How much money do you keep in that thing?" I asked him, nodding at the cumbersome safe.

"A few thousand," Tree said, a smile working at one corner of his mouth.

"A few thousand. A few thousand like thirty thousand? I figure that's the minimum you need on hand at a place like this. Or maybe I'm off a little, maybe it's twenty, twenty-five. But that kind of money."

"I do have that kind of money, here. But not in that safe."

"Where, then?"

He didn't answer immediately.

Then he evidently decided if he could trust his life to me, he could trust me with other things.

"There's a small floor vault under the carpet," he said. "In that corner over there."

"I guess you need to take some precautions, with a place stuck out here in the country like this, right? What other kind of security measures do you have? Besides that window behind you."

The window high on the wall behind Tree had a heavy metal grill on the outside and I assumed the glass to be shatterproof.

"I'm tied in with a security outfit in Des Moines," he said, "and with the police station, such as it is, in West Lake. Lights go on in both places if anybody tries to break in. We're five miles from West Lake. Fifteen from Des Moines. Takes four minutes for the West Lake man to get here. The security outfit, Vigilant Protective Service, can get here in twelve minutes. With the alarm system I got, nobody could get in and out with the money in that short a time."

"You seem pretty sure."

"So would you, if you had triple-bolted doors, alarms on all of them, on the windows too, and three back-up devices, including some in the floor of this room, under the carpet, that I switch on just as I'm leaving."

"You're usually the last one out of here?"

"Yeah. We close at two. It takes a while for the dealers to turn their money in, naturally. But by two-thirty, most nights, all the help's out of here, and I'm gone by two-thirty-seven. A few nights lately I been cutting out early, to see Ruthy. I got a guy upstairs in the kitchen who closes up for me on nights like that."

"What's your arrangement with your dealers? How much do you pay them?"

Tree shrugged. "Percentage of winnings. That's the only way to fly. Thirty percent, and that's good and goddamn generous, as a place like this goes."

"You start off each dealer with a set amount of cash, each night, then, which can be replenished if necessary . . ."

"Yeah, two thousand each, and that usually holds up, if they're any good."

"What if they aren't?"

"What?"

"Aren't any good? What if they lose?"

"If a guy has a bad week, I come through for him. It can happen to anybody. I help him out, lay a few hundred on 'im. I keep my people happy, and that way they don't try to pull anything on me."

"What if somebody consistently loses?"

"Then I fire his ass, of course. What's this all about?"

"The other night you said you were thinking of replacing a dealer. Did you say that just to have an excuse for giving me the job, or do you really have somebody worth getting rid of?"

"You tell me, Quarry. You played here for a week."

"Then I'd say it's the sour little asshole with the glasses. The college boy."

"I'd say you're right."

"He loses heavily?"

"Not really. But he doesn't win. He's been with me a couple of months. Did okay at first, then had a real bad night and I think it kind of threw him for a loop. He's never really recovered. He lost a few more times after that and then ever since he's been just sort of breaking even."

"He lost all the nights I played him."

"Not according to him. He's had at least two thousand to turn back in, at the end of the night."

"He's giving you money out of his own pocket, then."

"Why in hell would he do that?"

"To postpone the inevitable . . . his getting canned."

"It still doesn't make any sense. If he's losing, why would he want to hang onto his chair?"

"He could be a compulsive gambler, and's hoping to recoup. Or he could be somebody who's here to do something besides play cards."

"Oh. Jesus. Is *that* what he is?"

"Possibly. I don't know. I do know he's one of the guys who worked me over a few nights back. The other one's another college-boy type who's been a regular here. Blond-haired kid with big ears?"

"I think I know who you mean."

"Yeah, well the other night, before Lu and I joined you at DiPreta's, I had a little run-in with that clown. He was following me, and I suckered him into an alley and put him to sleep. Temporarily, that is. He drives a Chevelle. It's out in your lot right now. So is he, probably. I didn't see him upstairs or down, but that's no surprise. I broke his nose the other night and he probably doesn't want to show what's left of his face around here, where he might see me."

"Then why's he here at all?"

"I can think of a reason."

That stopped him for a moment.

"This is it, then," he said.

"Tonight's the night, you mean? Shit, I don't know.

There's too many things that just don't track here. I'm starting to think this is something else entirely."

"Like what?"

"I'm working on it. I think we better have an understanding. If I get involved in something that is apart from our other business together, but something that turns out to be of benefit to you, can I expect to be rewarded accordingly?"

"You bet your ass."

"Okay, then."

And I got up and went to the door.

Went out to gamble.

30

JOHN SMITH WAS sitting in the blue Chevelle, on the rider's side. Slouched against the door, smoking a cigarette, two fingers resting gingerly on his bandaged nose. Where surveillance was concerned, he'd been an incompetent agent, but you could hardly ask for a better subject. It was like sneaking up on a corpse.

The parking lot, dimly lit except directly under the small neon over the door, was empty of anything but cars at the moment. Ten o'clock was too late for many people to be arriving and too early for many people to be leaving. And a perfect time to go out to my GT on one side of the lot, unlock the glove compartment and get out the silenced nine-millimeter, and walk over to the other side of the lot and the Chevelle.

The door he was leaning against was unlocked, I noticed,

and when I opened it he fell out like an ironing board from its closet.

He had a gun, a Smith and Wesson snubnose .38, but it, like his cigarette, tumbled out of his fingers while he was tumbling out himself. I scooped up the .38, dropped it into a jacket pocket and pointed the nine-millimeter at the middle of his face.

He was sprawled on his right side and looked like he was trying to swim in the gravel. He looked comical. More so, when his eyes crossed to look at the barrel of the nine-millimeter.

"You motherfucker," he said, lamely, like he'd never used the word before in his life.

"Shhh," I said.

"What's going . . ."

I poked his nose with the gun's.

"Shhh, I said."

He put a hand over his nose. He started to weep.

"Please," I said. "This is embarrassing enough as it is."

I patted him down with my free hand. He had no other weapon.

"Keys," I said.

He pointed at the car.

I looked over and the keys were in the dash.

"Get them," I said.

He pushed himself up, hesitantly, and leaned into the car. I leaned in with him, pressing the flat snout of the silenced gun against his back, his ribs, and he got the keys. We leaned back out and he turned slowly and held out the keys to me. They dangled like a vulgar earring.

I didn't take them. I shut the car door and said, "Open the trunk."

He cocked his head, like he couldn't quite make out what

I was saying. With those ears of his, you'd think he wouldn't have any trouble hearing.

"The trunk," I said.

He shrugged, but the casualness of that gesture didn't work for him. This was one scared shitless character.

Which didn't keep him from opening the trunk, fumblingly of course, but he opened it.

I had, by this time, stuck the nine-millimeter in my waistband. For a guy like this I didn't need the gun. In fact I could've given it to him to hold for me.

I glanced around, looking for the beams of light that would indicate someone coming up the drive into the lot, looking to see if anyone was coming out a Barn door, or if anyone might be able to see us from a window. The latter was barely possible, but between the lack of windows downstairs and the shuttered ones upstairs, and our being way over to the far side of the lot, I felt it unlikely there were any eyes on us.

So we were standing in front of the trunk of the Chevelle like a couple of guys in front of an altar, or urinal. And my bland-looking college kid companion, with his busted nose and big, apparently nonfunctional ears, looked at me wondering what to do next. I told him.

"Get in," I said.

He cocked his head again.

"In," I said, and pointed at the trunk.

He cocked his head and pointed at the trunk with me.

"Oh Jesus," I said, and pushed him in there and shut the lid.

31

AFTER CLOSING I sat at the bar and nursed a gimlet while Lu was cleaning glasses and generally tidying up. The dealers were filing into Tree's office to turn in their money, and witness the ritual of seeing the money go in his fat relic of a safe. There was a second ritual, nightly, of the money being shifted to the real safe, the one in the floor under the carpet, but the dealers didn't get to see that.

The guy with glasses was one of the first to go, but the sound of the outer door opening and closing didn't follow him. I hadn't expected it to.

I waited till the line of dealers had thinned down to two, and went to the coat room to get my jacket. The .38 I'd lifted from the party currently residing in the trunk of a Chevelle was still in the pocket I'd dropped it in. I'd returned the bulky nine-millimeter to the GT's glove compartment. If Lu happened to see me with a gun, I'd prefer it was the .38 and not the silenced automatic, professional tool that the latter one was.

I went up the short flight of stairs to the landing that separated the club room of the Barn from the restaurant. Stairs rose from the landing a full flight, wide and without a rail, softly carpeted, to the wide doorless entry area of the dining room. I slipped the .38 out of the jacket pocket and started up.

The restaurant closed down at eleven, and all the help involved with that part of the Barn operation were long gone. The large rustic dining room, with its many booths, was dark. I didn't like that. Not at all. All those fucking booths, so many places to hide, Christ.

I stalked the room like a parody of a western gunfighter in this parody of a western setting. Winding through the rows of picket-fence booths, the thick carpet cushioning my steps, soaking up what little noise I made. Clint Eastwood would've been proud of me.

Then I saw the hairline of light beneath the door of the men's room.

Both of the johns were just off the top of the flight of stairs. An easy, logical place to duck into.

But the lack of imagination these guys showed was staggering. Not only was this asshole hiding in the john, an overly enclosed space and an obvious choice, and the men's john at that, but he'd even left the lights on. After all, who wants to wait around in the dark? Pathetic.

"Yeah, okay," I said loudly, in a lower voice that I hoped didn't sound like my own. "Be with you in a second, Frank. Just let me take a leak."

And I went in.

There was one booth, door closed, no feet showing below.

I stood at the urinal a few moments, flushed it, walked over and turned on the hot water in the sink, never turning my back completely to the booth, the door to which I then kicked open and the guy in there, standing and crouching at the same time on top of the stool, in an inane attempt not to be seen, caught the edge of the metal door on the chin and threw his head back against the cement wall and he then slid down and bumped every vertebra on his spine along the toilet's metallic spine from which extended the flush knob until his ass thudded against the floor and his head came to an abrupt rest against the porcelain bowl.

Still in his hand, though limply held, was another S & W .38, this one with a longer barrel, which was the first faint sign of professionalism I'd seen from this fuck-up pair. I kicked the gun into the corner and kicked him in the balls.

He said something that wasn't exactly a word, grabbing himself, and his eyes were huge and round behind glasses bent out of shape and hanging on his face like a modernistic sculpture.

I picked him up by the front of the shirt and stuffed his head in the toilet a while.

Backwards is a hard way to get dunked, and when I brought him back up he was choking and sputtering and seemed about to die. I waited a second till he was better and then dunked him again, but frontways this time, to try to avoid killing him.

When I let him up, I didn't let loose.

"Do you know what happens to guys that get in over their heads?" I said.

He was in no shape to say anything, but that was okay. I didn't want an answer.

I shoved him back in and this time worked the flush handle a few times. A dozen maybe.

151

"They drown," I said, letting him back up.

I lifted him off the floor and sat him on the stool. "Get your breath back," I said.

He sat there complying, chest heaving, water running off his face like he'd been out in the rain a day or two. His shirt was soaked halfway down. I was barely wet at all.

"Can I . . . can I . . . can I . . ."

"Can you what? Say it."

"Can I . . . get my . . . get my glasses." He pointed between his legs. His glasses had come off and were down in the toilet somewhere. I told him go ahead.

He reached down through his legs and fished around and finally came up with them. He bent the heavy metal frames around a little and they sat a little better on his face. Not much better. And as water-streaked as they were, I didn't know what good they were doing him.

"You can dry them off, if you like," I said.

He was still breathing hard, heaving his chest, and he was trembling, too, but somewhere in there I could make out he was also nodding. He took some toilet paper and wiped off the glasses.

"There's not going to be any cops," I said.

He just looked at me, his breath slowing down gradually.

"Just like there's not going to be any heist," I said.

He looked down. The floor was wet.

"You invested some time and some money, but you know how it goes. You can't win 'em all. Though at least you finally filled a flush, huh?"

"Very funny," he said.

"Hey, coming out alive is winning of a sort."

He looked up. "Where's Johnny?"

"Johnny Smith, you mean? Big ears, nothing between? In the trunk of his Chevelle."

"Is he . . ."

"He's alive, if you call that living."

"What . . . what happens now?"

"Now you leave. You go out and get in your friend's Chevelle and drive away. Let him out of the trunk, when you get around to it."

I handed him the keys.

"You can have your gun, too," I said, and went over and picked it up. Stuck the other .38 in my waistband and emptied the shells of first one gun, then the other, into the used towel bin. Then I gave him both guns and he looked at me puzzled.

"That box of slugs in your glove compartment isn't there anymore, in case you're wondering. Even if it was, it wouldn't do you much good. Ask your friend about the gun I almost used on him and see if he'd like to go up against it."

"Why are you doing this?"

"Stopping the heist? I'm getting paid to."

"Why let us go, I mean."

"Because you're just not worth killing . . . though if I ever see you again, I'll have to reassess that. I'm not real fond of people who break lamps in my face, you know."

"You won't see me again. Don't worry about that."

"Oh I'm not worried Go away."

32

LU WAS SITTING at a table near the bar, waiting for me. "Where you been?" she wanted to know, She looked tired, but good. She always looked good.

"The john," I said.

I'd had my jacket on upstairs and it was all that got noticeably wet. It was now folded over my arm.

"Tree still in his office?" I asked her.

"Yeah. Expecting you, I guess."

"This won't take long. You don't mind waiting?"

"How can I mind?" she said, with a wry grin. "We came in one car, remember?"

Tree's door was open.

I closed it behind me.

"This room soundproof?" I asked.

"Yeah," he said, from behind his desk, "or damn near."

"Let's pretend it isn't."

I pulled the chair around by him and leaned head to head with him and spoke very softly.

"I took the liberty of firing your dealer at table four," I said. "He and his friend with the Chevelle were planning to heist you tonight."

He showed his teeth, but he wasn't smiling. "I figured as much, after thinking over what we talked about before. You got rid of them, then? How?"

"Took their guns away, put a little scare into 'em. They won't be back."

"That irritates the fuck out of me. How do you like those little sons of bitches? Little son of a bitch, after he lost big that one time, must've figured I'd fire him if he ever did again . . . brings in a friend and they feed some of their own money into holding onto the seat at that table, figuring to rip me off and get their money back and mine, too, little bastards . . ."

"And they might've done it."

"Those little turds? Why . . ."

"Why not? You mean if they stuck a gun in your nuts, you wouldn't tell them about your floor safe? They're idiots in a lot of ways, but just the same they put a lot into this, both money and time and even some thought. They figured out the weakness of your security set-up, which is those few minutes after closing, after all or anyway most of the dealers are gone, when you're here alone, with none of the alarm systems turned on. Which is something you might want to do something about sometime."

"Why'd they rough you up that time?"

"Maybe to get back six hundred bucks I won off them. Maybe they wondered if you were onto them somehow, and wanted to see if you planted me at the table, to keep an eye on them. It's also possible one of them saw me approach you that first time in the parking lot."

"You saved me a lot of money tonight, Quarry."

"Hey, I saved your ass. They could've killed you. At the least they'd caused some wear and tear."

"It's hard to put a price on something like that, isn't it?"

"Let's try."

He smiled on half his face and leaned over and swung open the door of the big safe. He took out every packet of money in there, six packets in all, and stacked them on the desk in front of me.

"Three thousand. Above and beyond our other arrangement. Speaking of which . . ." He opened a desk drawer and took out a check and put it on top of the stacked money packets. "The first thousand I owe you. Made out as you instructed."

"Good," I said. "Now. I want you to do something."

"What?"

"Don't go home tonight. Don't talk to anyone. That includes that cunt of yours."

"Ruthy? But . . ."

"Especially Ruthy."

"What are you talking about?"

"Ruthy is a good friend of Lu's."

"So what?"

"You gave Lu the bartender job because Ruthy asked you to, isn't that right? Because they were old friends?"

"Yes, yes, but what's that supposed to mean?"

"Lu is half the hit team, Frank."

"She's what . . . ?"

"You heard me."

"How long have you known this?"

"All along. I followed her here from Florida. Do you know where she lives, Frank?"

"Yes . . . yes I do . . ."

"Where, Frank?"

"Across the street from me."

"Who found her the apartment, Frank?"

"I think Ruthy did."

"That's right, Frank."

He kind of flopped back in his chair. His eyes were glazed, empty, like glass eyes.

Then he sat forward and said, "But, Christ, man . . . you're living with her . . . sleeping with her . . ."

"Which just goes to show you can't trust everybody you sleep with."

"How can you . . ."

"Hey, what better way to keep track of the situation, huh?"

"She could kill you."

"I could kill her."

"You're pretty goddamn fucking sure of yourself."

"She wouldn't kill me unless she was sure she needed to. People in this line of work aren't frivolous about killing. She was hired to do you in, not me, and unless she's sure I'm in her way, she wouldn't consider it. Especially in an apartment she rented herself."

"This is crazy . . ."

"Right. Anyway, drive someplace. Fifty miles away from here, or more. Check into a motel. You can come back to work tomorrow, and I'll see you here, tell you where we stand. Till then, don't be anywhere."

"I don't understand."

"Listen, I thought I had a handle on this. I thought I knew who the two people were that had your number, and that one of them was that little dealer of yours, with the glasses. Only he isn't, he's just some little jerk planning some little heist, so all bets are off, and I got to rethink this whole fucking deal, because I only know now for sure one of the two people who're here to cancel your subscriptions to those girlie magazines there. Now that makes me nervous. It ought to make you more than that. Go home tonight and maybe you don't wake up in the morning. Well?"

"I'll do what you say."

"Fine. Got a gun to take along?"

"Yes."

"Good. See you tomorrow night."

The pockets of the jacket were dry, and I stuffed half the packets of money into each pocket, tucked them down deep, and put the check in my billfold.

Then I carefully folded the jacket over my arm and went out and smiled at Lu, who rose from the table, hooked her arm in mine, and we drove back to Des Moines, to the apartment, and made love and fell asleep in each other's arms.

33

THE NEW PLAY opened tonight at the Candle Lite Playhouse, and the marquee had been changed accordingly. It was early afternoon and the block's worth of parking lot adjacent to the big brick two-story was empty. I parked along the side of the building, with a few other cars; Christine Price and a couple other people had apartments here in the theater building, and the cars probably belonged to them.

I'd spent a leisurely morning at the apartment. Lu slept in till damn near noon. I was awake around seven and sat drinking Sanka, watching the morning game shows and soap operas on the portable, volume turned down low. I watched the shows but didn't watch them. Thinking is what I did. A lot of thinking.

Then when Lu woke up, I fixed a late breakfast for us.

She appreciated that. She said it took a liberated man to work in the kitchen. I said it took a bachelor. As we ate I told her I had another job interview this afternoon, and she said fine and didn't ask for particulars, which was nice of her, as it saved me the trouble of making some up.

There was no problem getting inside at the Candle Lite. The front doors were unlocked, just like the other day. Beyond the front doors, to the left off an entry landing, some stairs led down. Some other stairs, a shorter flight, went up to the lobby. I climbed them, wondering if strike weekend was over.

It seemed to be. The stage set was finished, four-poster bed and other antique furniture assembled into a bedroom, the walls of which were painted and made very realistic-looking scenery. No one was on stage. No one was in the big theater room with its gentle tiers with the small covered tables with chairs.

I walked back out into the lobby and down to the entryway, only I turned left this time, headed on down the stairs to the lower level, where Ruthy's apartment was.

The big room still looked like the basement it was. Besides a few clusters of stage props, battered furniture, dressing screens, and so on, the room was just a spacious, open area probably used as a rehearsal hall. One large corner of the room, however, was walled off, and considering the size of the place the walled-off area was the size of a small house.

Ruthy's house.

There was a door, with a glittery star on it. A sarcastic comment on the fact that an actress lived within. At least I thought it was meant to be a sarcastic comment. With Ruthy, who could say?

I knocked.

It didn't take her long to answer.

She was wearing a red terry cloth robe, but the terry cloth was-brushed or cut some way that made it look like velvet. It was long and flowing, but it clung to her, was belted around her middle and the neckline plunged. Of course.

She touched her hair, which was piled up on top of her head recklessly, and she said, "You really don't believe in giving a girl much notice, do you? Come on in."

She led me through, a small living room that looked like a prop room, odd pieces of secondhand furnishings scattered around with no apparent plan, and ranging from a possibly antique love seat to a cigar-store Indian with his cigars broken off. From the living room we passed through a small kitchenette area, just large enough for a table and chairs, refrigerator, stove and sink, and a lot of dirty dishes. Then we were in a tiny hall, about the size of a broom closet, off of which was a surprisingly large bath room on the one side, and her bedroom on the other, the latter being where we finally ended up.

There were only three things in the room: her round bed, with pink sheets and a fuzzy white something spread, unmade; a huge wardrobe trunk, standing open, like a mouth going sideways, with various clothes hanging and drawers that her other things were apparently stored in; and an imposing dressing-room-style dresser with big square mirror surrounded by glowing dwarf light bulbs. The top of the dresser was cluttered with various sorts of make-up, and on the walls around the mirror, and elsewhere in the room but not as concentrated as here, were pictures of her, both glossy posed photos with the crest of a studio photographer, and large color blow-ups of snapshots taken during various performances of plays she'd been in.

She sat in front of the mirror and started taking some pins out of her hair.

"Make yourself comfortable," she said. "You want something to eat? I can fix us something. You rather wait till afterwards, for that?"

"Is that why you think I'm here?" I said, sitting on the round bed. "To fuck you?"

She shook her head, not in any response to me, but to make her blond hair tumble to her shoulders, which it did, as if in slow motion. Her smile in the mirror was as smug as it was sexual.

"Why else?" she said. "You knew it was here if you wanted it. And I knew you'd come and get it, sooner or later."

"Why's that?"

"Because this is exciting to you. You're shacked up with my best friend . . . who'd scratch my eyes out if she knew, and yours too, probably. And I'm seeing your new boss . . . who happens to be the type who frowns on somebody messing with his property. I think all of that's kind of exciting, don't you?"

"I get chills."

She dropped her robe to her waist. Cupped her big, small-pointed breasts and looked at them appraisingly in the mirror. Then she took some lipstick and touched it against each nipple, rubbed the dark red rouge into each nipple with the forefinger of either hand, then licked each finger.

I'd had this wrong, from the first day, and there was no excuse for it. I'd made an assumption I shouldn't have and I was an asshole for it. I had assumed that simply because she was a woman, Lu would naturally play the stakeout role, the passive part.

But I knew now I was wrong.

Lu played the same role I used to play, when I was in the business: she killed people.

And her back-up man had almost as big a tits as she did.

"You've traveled around a lot, haven't you, Ruthy? Played a lot of dinner theaters, all over the country?"

"Sure," she said. She was using some kind of tiny black pencil or crayon or something to draw a star-shaped beauty mark to the right of the nipple of her left breast.

"And when you appear in a play, you might stay in a town as long as six weeks, or two months maybe?"

"That's right," she said, idly.

"Plenty long enough to strike up a relationship with a gentleman friend."

She gave me that schoolgirl smile of hers, but it dissipated into a smirk as she said, "I've been known to know a man now and again."

"You could get to know a man pretty well in that space of time. Know just about his every habit, whole pattern of his life."

She shrugged, stood, and let the robe drop to the floor. She had a great ass. Her thighs in back looked smooth, slippery, but firm; her calves were muscular, tapering. She turned and rubbed her breasts, smearing the lipstick but leaving the little black star intact and then kind of scratched at her snatch and said, "I'm gonna have a bath," and hip-swayed out of the room.

I heard the bath water drawing.

I walked across the nothing hall and into the large bathroom. She was leaning over testing the water as it came out of the faucet. She poured in some milky bubble bath.

There was a counter-top sink, with more make-up and feminine things and another big mirror. There was also a small portable television on the edge of the counter, for her to watch as she bathed.

"Know what a black widow is?" I asked her.

"Sure," she said, getting in, water still flowing, bubble bath bubbling up, "it's a female spider that eats her mate. Why? You want eaten?"

"Don't get me wrong, now," I said, putting down the lid on the stool and sitting, "I'm not comparing you to a black widow. You don't kill your men. You just set them up for it."

A hardening around and in her eyes, very slight, told me she had caught on, for the first time, to what this conversation was about. Till now, she thought it was all some kind of coy sexual ritual, some verbal foreplay thing I was engaging in.

But she didn't change her style.

"When I get done in this tub," she said, taking some soap and soaping between her legs, "I can love you to death, if you want, honey."

"I don't want. But there's something I do want."

"Oh?"

"I want to know whether you picked up your money yet."

"Huh?" She turned off the water. She slid down under the surface so that bubbles covered-her, except for her lipstick-painted breasts, which bobbled surrealistically on the water.

"I said I want to know whether you picked up the money. "

"What money?" she said.

"If you picked up the money, I want to know where and when. If you haven't yet, well, have you?"

"Jack, I really don't know what you're talking about."

Standard operating procedure, back when I was working with the Broker, was for the middle man to accept twenty-five percent down, from whoever was buying the contract. The balance was picked up by the back-up man, the passive half of the team, just a day or so prior to the actual hit; and that was the only contact (and an indirect contact at that, since it amounted to going to a drop point and picking up the cash) the hitmen had with whoever hired them.

Ruthy knew this, and I knew she did.

I turned on the portable TV.

"What are you doing?" she said.

"Turning on the TV," I said. "What does it look like I'm doing? Say, Ruthy, tell me . . . you're in show biz. Which soap opera is that that's on? I can't tell them apart. Is it *One Life to Live*, or *Another World* or what?"

"Jack . . ."

"You know it's dangerous having something electrical like this in bathroom. It could fall off into the tub. Oh, but I see you have the cord knotted up, so if that happens the set would unplug itself. That's smart thinking, Ruthy. Here. I'll just unplug it for a minute and unwind this cord and, hey it's nice and long isn't it? Just plug it in again and there's your soap opera back. You don't mind if I keep the volume down while we talk?"

"Jack, I'm getting out."

"No," I said. "You just stay put."

"Jack . . ."

"Stay put," I said.

I was standing over her, holding the set by the handle on top, holding the plug in the wall socket with my free hand, while silent images of a man and a woman arguing, their faces in close-up, flickered across the screen. I held the set over the water, right above her lap, and said, "What about the money?"

"Jack, let me get out. We'll go in the bedroom and I'll make you real happy, Jack, God I'm good, Jack, look at *these*, Jack, Jack, look at *me*, you'd like it in me . . ."

"The money. Where. When."

"I . . . I made the pick-up yesterday."

Shit. I'd hoped she hadn't made it yet, so I could make her lead me to the pick-up when it was made and I could find out who had hired Tree dead.

"Where?" I said.

"Iowa City," she said.

"Iowa City?"

"Yes, in an alley, in a trashcan downtown. Jack. Jack, can I get out now?"

"You just sit there a minute."

"If you let me out of here, Jack, I won't say a word about this, I won't mention this to Lucille, if you want, I'd even help you get rid of her, Jack, anything, anything you want."

"Ruthy."

"Jack?"

"For once I don't think you're acting," I said, and tossed in the TV.

34

ALONG ONE SIDE of the Psychopathic Hospital was a sun porch. Despite the massive iron doors that Tree and I had been buzzed through the other day, security here was nonexistent. Most of the patients at the hospital had signed themselves in, and were free to go when they chose to, theoretically anyway. I assumed there were some sections of the hospital where patients were in fact kept under lock and key. But the ward where Frank Tree, Jr., was staying was not a prison, nor a collection of padded cells. It was simply a sort of dormitory with doctors.

At least there were supposed to be doctors there. I'd seen just one, last visit, and then only fleetingly. The nurses had been kids of either sex in street clothes and with expressions as spacey as the patients, who had themselves been a scarce commodity around there Monday.

Tree had explained that many of the patients were involved in one supervised activity or another, elsewhere in the building, afternoons.

All of which should make it easy for me to do what I had to.

I hoped.

The afternoon was shadowy with moving clouds, and the air was chill. Spring was supposed to be here any second now, but you could've fooled me.

But you couldn't have fooled Roger. He alone was sitting out on the sun porch, enjoying the moody, overcast day, with the innocence that allows the retarded to find joy in joyless things.

He was wearing the same outfit as last time: gray IOWA tee-shirt, baggy brown slacks, enormous white tennis shoes. The slack expression on his irregularly featured face turned into a grin as he saw me approaching the porch. He shook a cue stick of a finger at me, trying to place me. Some sounds came out of his mouth and they had a vague resemblance to words.

I went up the few steps and Roger, who had been swinging in the porchswing, stood and towered over me like a gorilla in a person suit.

"Hello, Roger. How are you? How is Frank Jr.?"

He thought that over for a minute or two, and then something not unlike awareness glimmered in those oddly compelling green eyes of his. He grasped my wrist, which for him was like holding a pencil in his fist, and led me through a screen door and into a hallway. I recognized it as the same hallway as the other day, and the same bored-looking nurse moved briskly by us, with clipboard in hand, paying no attention to either one of us.

Roger stopped outside the door of the room where Frank

Jr. had one of six beds. Roger put a finger to his lips and said, "Seeeep."

"Right," I said.

Then I leaned into the room and saw what he meant. Frank Jr. was on his back sleeping, or anyway resting, on one of the beds, head settled against the pillow with the word PSYCHO on it. He wasn't wearing a robe today. He had on a yellow tee-shirt and jeans. He was alone in the room.

"I won't disturb him," I whispered.

Roger was still holding onto my wrist.

"I'll sit with him till he wakes up, and then I'll talk to him."

Roger thought.

"Go back out on the porch now, Roger."

And he nodded, dropped my wrist like a stone and shuffled away.

And I made damn sure he was out the door, before going in and taking Frank Jr. by the shoulder and shaking him.

"Wake up," I said, several times.

He finally did.

He looked so much like his father it was spooky. The smaller, slightly feminine nose and the long dark black hair remained the only differences. Tree must've looked much the same at eighteen or nineteen.

"You don't know who I am," I said. "And you don't need to know, other than I'm somebody trying to find out why you paid to have your father killed."

He narrowed his eyes, just a little, and got upon his elbows, but said nothing.

"Now he's not dead yet, don't misunderstand. Today was supposed to be the day, I think, but I doubt it'll come off. Of course I don't expect you to say anything, but I do expect you to listen. I'm not a cop, nothing remotely like a cop. You aren't in any danger of exposure any other way, either. I work for your father, you saw me here with him the other day, but I know him well enough to figure he's not going to buy it when I tell him his own kid wants him wasted."

Maybe that was a faint smile on the kid's face; or maybe it was just the shadows from the clouds outside, coming in the window, filling this overcast room with more of the same.

"Your father told me all about how you have this habit of, wherever you go, falling in with bad company . . . but like most fathers he can't conceive of his son being bad company. I think it's just as funny as you probably do, that he really thinks he saved you in the nick of time, from the horrors of addiction. . . . He actually thinks he stumbled onto that heroin stash minutes before you were to put a match under a spoon of the stuff and fill your hypo and stick it in and another hopeless junkie is born. He was so goddamn relieved when he brought you here and you weren't hooked on anything stronger than grass. I guess there really is such a thing as a generation gap. You and your old man make your money different ways, that's all, and he runs a gambling house but he gambles himself, so he finds it hard to understand that a guy who deals in dope rarely uses himself. Especially the hard stuff. Or maybe he can't see that just because you're his kid . . . won't let himself see it, maybe."

Yes it was a smile. Faint, but a smile.

"When he told me about the quantities of grass and H he found in your room, and your car, I figured he was just exaggerating, remembering through his emotions. But when I thought about it, it made sense. . . . You had junk in quantity because you're a dealer. A major dealer, maybe . . . maybe dealing to dealers. Something. How much heroin did he flush down the john? Hundred thousand bucks worth, maybe? That *would* hurt. No wonder you got pissed at Pop. And then he starts this half-ass citizens' group, and hurts business even more, and embarrasses you in the eyes of the people you deal with, above you and below you both. I mean, shit. A kid can only take so much."

He was sitting up, now, and his smile was gone. He wasn't back doing his catatonic act, though; he was pretending to be bored, or maybe he just was.

"Little towns are where a lot of the major dope deals go down these days, am I right? We're talking about distribution on pretty large scale, I'd guess. Too much heat in the bigger cities for that anymore. I'd bet West Lake was where you were making your drops, not Des Moines. How long you been in the business? Since you were fifteen? Thirteen? What the fuck. The old man'd be proud of you. He taught you the importance of money, and how you ought to hustle it up for yourself. You were a hell of a student, too. But my one question is this, junior. Did somebody bigger than you tell you the old man had to go? Or did you decide that yourself?"

And he spoke.

He said, "Blow it out your ass."

"Thanks," I said. "That's all I wanted to know."

It had been sheer speculation up to this point; but once Frank Jr. opened his trap, all suspicions were confirmed.

He rolled over on his side, away from me.

I took him by the arm and pulled him over, made him face me.

"I took a chance coming here," I said "But I had to find out. And I did, and you're coming with me."

171

"You came, to the right place, asshole," he said. "Because you are out of your fuck-ing mind."

"Maybe so, but I'm still not crazy enough to think I can convince your dear old daddy that junior wants to make him dead old daddy. But *you* could do it. Not willingly, but with you there to have to try and knock down my story, well, it's going to be worth a try."

"What the fuck's it to you?"

"Five thousand dollars."

"Aw, Christ, I can get you that. I can get you more."

"Sorry. That'd be unethical. Besides, I don't like to work for anybody who hasn't gone through puberty yet. Also, I got this aversion to father killers. Call me picky, if you like, but we all got our little quirks."

"I'm not going with you."

"I think you will. I got a roll of nickels in my jacket pocket, here, that's going to be in my hand when I hit you, if you make me. Not the latest in anesthetics, but it'll do. Or we could go to the doctors and tell them you want 'em to contact your father, so you can talk to him. That's okay with me, too. Up to you."

"And suppose I just tell them you're some fucking crank and they should throw you the fuck out of here."

"I don't think they'll do that to the miracle man who gave you back the gift of speech, now, do you? So come on. Let's just walk out the side door, to my car, and we'll go see what's happening back in Des Moines."

I let go of his arm and he got off the bed and slid onto the floor, and I turned a little to let him by me and then the little bastard was on me, tight little hands on my throat, and I was going over on my back, landing hard on the cold tile floor, and he was on top of me, squeezing my throat, fingernails digging in, and he wasn't particularly strong but he'd got me by surprise and had dug in good before I got my arms out from under him and punched him on one ear, which shook him, and he let go of my throat but one hand found its way into my hair, which he proceeded to pull, and his other hand was a fist, hammering me in the upper chest. I was trying to slide my hand inside my jacket pocket, to get that roll of nickels and give him a shot that'd put him out now, when the sound of a groan filled the room, that might have been a moose in heat or King Kong annoyed or Roger.

Roger, coming across the room faster than he should've been able to.

And then he was lifting Frank Jr. off of me, pulling Frank Jr. off, and squeezed him, protectively, the grotesque features of his face twisted with concern, confusion, excitement, and as he squeezed Frank Jr. I heard things snapping, like twigs, popping, like flashbulbs, and as I saw the boy go limp and his head roll back, showing large lifeless eyes looking at nothing, I realized the snapping twigs and popping bulbs were the things inside Frank Jr. that held him together, that made the machine of his body function, but this was something Roger didn't realize, and he kept hugging the boy.

Boy did he hug him.

And suddenly there wasn't anything left to do but try to get out of there before Roger looked for someone else to turn his attention to.

35

WHEN I GOT back, she wasn't there. It was evening now, close to seven, and maybe she was at the Barn, behind the bar, making drinks for people.

I doubted it. With Ruthy dead, Lu would be leaving town, maybe already had. Hitting Tree now would be out of the question. Her back-up "man" gone, possibly murdered, Lu had no choice but get the hell out.

You just don't hang around when a job goes sour, and it can't go much more sour than your partner getting electrocuted in a bathtub.

But when I looked in the closet, her things were still there. It was a relief and a disappointment. A relief because the notion of maybe seeing her again was something I hadn't been able to let go of yet; a disappointment because I'd tried to work this thing around so that she'd be forced out of it. She was supposed to be gone.

The phone was on the wall in the kitchenette. The dirty dishes from the late breakfast I'd fixed were still in the sink. I called the Barn and asked for her. She wasn't there. I wondered whether that was good or bad, then asked to be put through to Tree.

I wondered if he'd heard about his kid yet.

"Quarry . . . where the fuck are you?"

So he hadn't heard. After all, I'd told him to hole up in a motel all day somewhere, and he hadn't been at the Barn for more than an hour or so probably, and Iowa City evidently hadn't tracked him down yet. Well, I wasn't about to break the news.

"Des Moines," I said. "I won't be coming out tonight. I'm leaving."

"There were a couple of cops, just here. . . . They left not five minutes ago. I don't have to tell you what they were doing here, do I?"

"No."

"Did you have to . . . to do that to her, Quarry? My God . . . I . . . I thought a lot of that little girl, I thought she was . . . I just can't . . . my first reaction was I wanted your goddamn throat in my hands, but . . . if she was what you say she was, Jesus. It's hard to accept . . . but I suppose it had to be done."

"That's right."

"And I suppose an . . . accident is, uh, better than . . ."

"That's right."

"I notice I'm missing a lady bartender tonight."

"You better replace her."

"I see. So. You're leaving. That means you weren't able to do anything about finding who was responsible. . . ?"

"I found out."

"Well, shit, man, who? And what's to be done?"

"It's been done. You're better off not knowing the details,

but I'll tell you this. . . . It was someone very close to your son, involved in this narcotics thing just like you imagined."

"And you've taken care of the son of a bitch?"

"He's been taken care of."

"Knowing the kind of work you do, Quarry, I'll just bet he has. Look, I got another call coming in on my other line. . . ."

"You know where to send the money."

"I'll do it. And thanks, Quarry."

"Yeah."

I put the receiver back, wondering if that incoming call was Iowa City finally getting hold of him. And then Lu came home.

36

SHE CAME IN and sat on the couch. She seemed a little depressed. She was wearing that dark brown pants suit again. She slipped the jacket off and draped it over the coffee table and stretched, breasts straining at the yellow-and-tan stripe halter top.

"I heard about Ruthy," I said, "Tree told me. I'm sorry."

"Yeah. It's got me a little upset. I knew her for a long time." She shook her head, put her feet on the table. "Well. I wasn't expecting to see you here. I thought you'd be at the Barn, breaking in your table."

"I just called Tree and quit . . . if you can quit a job before you start. You know that interview today? Got the job on the spot."

"I'm glad, Jack. That's such good news. I'm quitting myself. . . . After what happened to Ruthy, I just don't feel like staying around this town anymore."

"Yeah, well. I can't blame you."

"When are you leaving?"

"Tonight. Right away. Got to be in Wisconsin tomorrow morning."

"I think I'll take off tonight, myself. Back to Florida."

"I guess we both better start packing, then."

"I guess. I guess I ought to change into something I can drive in, huh?"

She stood and undressed and let her clothes fall to the floor in a heap, and I took a long, memorizing look at that body. Then she went over and turned off the lights and went back to the couch and lay down and held out her arms to me.

We humped like a couple of teenagers in the back of a car, with a desperate, innocent horniness, as we might have if we'd met a long time ago, when we were different people. And I was still on top of her, still inside her, both of us breathing hard, sweating together, when I said, "Come with me."

"Seems to me I just did."

"You know what I mean, Lu."

"Jack . . . thank you, Jack. Maybe . . . next time."

We left the dirty dishes behind, and she got in her Stingray and followed me to the Interstate. She turned one way and I turned the other.

Maybe next time.

Afterword

THIS IS THE third novel about my hitman hero Quarry, and it's always been one of my favorites. I think it's probably the best of the original four, although *Quarry*, the first book, has an integrity and freshness that no sequel can match. Still, as a series entry, *Quarry's Deal* is a good example of what I was trying to accomplish.

The title of the novel's original publication was *The Dealer*. This was my title, and I still like it. But I came up with it to try to fit a pattern created by some unknown editor at Berkley Books in the mid-1970s who decided to publish my novel *Quarry* as *The Broker* and its sequel as *The Broker's Wife* (my title had been *Hit List*, and the book is now known as *Quarry's List*) (available from Perfect Crime).

Donald E. Westlake, who was such an influence on both my Nolan and Quarry novels, revealed to me at the time that his title for the Parker novel *The Rare Coin Score* had been *The Dealer*. That seemed fitting somehow.

Anyway, Quarry was just a busted four-book paperback series from the '70s, as far as I was concerned, and I had gone on about my business, writing other stuff, including the *Dick Tracy* comic strip. That the Quarry books had appeared and sunk like stones disappointed me, because I thought the concept and the character were strong, and reflected me at my best, at that stage anyway. The series had the potential to take off, but the publisher had blown it.

All writers feel this way about their work, however, so even I didn't take such thoughts very seriously. We had a few nice reviews here and there (thank you, Jon Breen), but mostly the books were just cannon fodder . . . grist for the publishing mill.

So it was a pleasant surprise to have a cult following grow up around the character. I began getting mail in the late '70s, and this continued well into the '80s. The books became known enough by 1985 for a mystery specialist publisher, Foul Play Press, to bring out the first four books and commission a new one. All five of these have gone out of print and are now as rare as the original Berkley Books paperbacks. I'm pleased that John Boland's Perfect Crime is bringing the first five books out again.

One of the reasons why I like this book is the notion of Quarry meeting up with a female version of himself. Talk about true love. I didn't know whether he would wind up killing Lu or not—I always know the workings of the mysteries in the Quarry novels, but never plan how Quarry will behave in the final showdown (he's an excitable boy, as Warren Zevon put it). So I was pleased he didn't kill her. I may still bring her back, if this cult enthusiasm continues. Or are you people just screwing with me?

MAX ALLAN COLLINS
August 2010

About the Author

Max Allan Collins, who created the graphic novel on which the Oscar-winning film *Road to Perdition* was based, has been writing hard-boiled mysteries since his college days in the Writers Workshop at the University of Iowa. Besides the books about killer-for-hire Quarry, he has written a popular series of historical mysteries featuring Nate Heller and many, many other novels. At last count, Collins's books and short stories have been nominated for fifteen Shamus awards by the Private Eye Writers of America, winning for two Heller novels, *True Detective* and *Stolen Away*. He lives in Muscatine, Iowa with his wife, Barbara Collins, with whom he has collaborated on several novels and numerous short stories. The photo above shows Max in 1971, when he created Quarry.

Made in the USA
San Bernardino, CA
02 April 2015